FIVE WILL GET YOU . . . DEAD!

Clint had a feeling that whatever happened once the action started, the two brothers would run into the other room for their guns. He'd have to catch them before they got to them.

"Kenny . . ." Clint said.

"I'm thinking!" Brett snapped. His hand flexed around the gun nervously, again and again. At one point, for an instant, his trigger finger was out of position for an easy pull. Clint kept his eyes on the boy's hands. . . . "You can't draw on me and win . . . you can't," Brett said.

"Don't make me prove it, boy," Clint said. "Put the gun down."

Brett licked his lips and looked at the Davis boys. In that moment, Clint drew. . . .

THE GUNSMITH

209

DEATH TIMES FIVE

J. R. ROBERTS

JOVE BOOKS, NEW YORK

DEATH TIMES FIVE

A Jove Book / published by arrangement with
the author

PRINTING HISTORY
Jove edition / June 1999

The Penguin Putnam Inc. World Wide Web site address is
http://www.penguinputnam.com

ISBN: 0-515-12520-2

A JOVE BOOK®
Jove Books are published by The Berkley Publishing Group,
a division of Penguin Putnam Inc.,
375 Hudson Street, New York, New York 10014.
JOVE and the "J" design
are trademarks belonging to Penguin Putnam Inc.

PRINTED IN THE UNITED STATES OF AMERICA

10 9 8 7 6 5 4 3 2 1

THE GUNSMITH

209

DEATH TIMES FIVE

PROLOGUE

They called him Cherry Boy because when he joined them he had never raped or killed anyone.

That was about to change.

All five of them were nineteen years old, four of them with more experience than most nineteen-year-olds had.

"We have to do this tonight?" Cherry Boy asked, nervously.

Rufus King, the leader of the gang, slapped Cherry Boy on the back and said, "Sooner we bust that cherry of yours the better, boy!"

"You wanna be one of us, don't ya?" Lucky Davis asked.

"Well, sure—"

"Well, this'll do it for ya," Louis Davis, Lucky's brother, said. "This'll do it for sure."

The five of them looked at the small, well-lit house that was just outside Muskogee, Oklahoma. Rufus had checked it out. He knew that the family that lived there had a mother and father and two brats.

"How do you know they'll do what they're told?" Cherry Boy asked.

1

"When there's brats involved," Rufus said, "the folks usually do what they're told to do."

"But—"

"Come on," Rufus said, dismounting. "We got to go up to the house on foot or they'll hear us."

The Davis brothers and Sam Sampson dismounted. Cherry Boy did so last, hesitantly.

"It's natural to be nervous the first time," Sampson said to him. "It'll pass once you get started."

"Got to bust that cherry," Rufus said, "and there's no time like the present."

"C'mon." Sampson put his arm firmly around Cherry Boy's shoulders to bring him along. "It's time to do it."

Rufus Buck led the way to the house, with the Davis boys trotting anxiously behind him. Behind them, Sam Sampson still had a firm hold on Cherry Boy and was bringing him along. As they approached the house Rufus and the Davis boys drew their guns. The Davis boys positioned themselves at the front door while Rufus peeked in a window. After a nod from Rufus, Lucky Davis raised his foot and kicked in the door. The door not only opened, but the flimsy wood splintered, a crack working its way right through the center of it.

Lucky and his brother went in first, followed by Rufus, and then Sampson and Cherry Boy.

When they got inside Lucky Davis was standing with his foot on a man's throat. The man was lying on the floor, bleeding from a wound to his scalp.

Standing next to the table was a woman in a gingham dress with two small children clinging to her legs. She was in her thirties, not pretty, but she had large, round breasts and full hips.

"Whoa," Rufus said, "this one's got a woman's body, yes sir."

"What are you—" the man tried to say from the floor, but Lucky increased the pressure of his boot on the man's throat, producing a gagging sound.

"Don't hurt my children," the woman said.

Sam Sampson and Louis Davis thought the woman was old and ugly. Rufus, more mature although the same age, could see the benefit of a woman's body. He liked large breasts on his women, and this woman had them.

Lucky Davis was too busy enjoying the feel of the man beneath his boot to notice the woman.

Cherry Boy thought she was pleasant-looking. He preferred women without all that face paint that the gals in the saloons wore, but he wished he could see this woman in one of those saloon-hall dresses. Her skin was pale, and he could imagine what she would have looked like in one of those dresses, her breasts spilling out.

"Look at Cherry Boy," Rufus said to the others. "He likes her."

"Wha—what do you want?" the woman quavered.

"Our friend here ain't never had him a woman," Rufus said. "You're gonna be his first."

"You can't—" Her husband tried to speak again, but the result was the same: Lucky's heavy foot on his neck.

"Mister," Lucky said, "you keep fussin', I'm gonna have to crush your throat with my heel."

"No!" the woman said. "I . . . I'll do what you want. Don't hurt him."

"Where's your room?" Rufus asked.

"There," she said, pointing.

"You go in there with our friend Cherry Boy, and you show him a good time, maybe we'll let your husband up off the floor."

"My children . . ."

"What about them?"

"Can they go to their room?"

Rufus looked at the two kids. One was a boy, and one was a girl, and to him they looked about the same age as his little brother, four or five.

"Okay," Rufus said. "We don't want them gettin' in the way, anyway."

"Go to your room, children," the woman said, shooing them that way.

"We didn't finish our dinner," the boy said.

"You'll finish after . . . our guests leave."

"They ain't guests," the little girl said, "they're bad men."

"It'll be all right," their mother said. "Go on."

Reluctantly, the two children went to their room.

"And close the door!" Rufus shouted.

They slammed it and he chuckled.

"Okay, missy," he said, "in ya go. G'wan, Cherry Boy, she's all yours."

Cherry Boy's penis was swelling so much that he thought he might not last until he got his pants off. He'd touched and been touched a few times with a neighbor girl, and one time his penis had just exploded, shooting white "nasty" stuff—the girl said—all over them. She never came back after that, and used to laugh behind her hand with her friends whenever they saw him in school. That was why he stopped going.

But even though she had called it "nasty," it had felt awfully good, so he had repeated the experience several times by himself. He knew what could happen, and he was afraid he might explode just while he was taking off his pants.

"Lookit Cherry Boy," Lucky Davis said. "He got him a tent in his pants."

"This lady is gonna take care of that for him, ain'tcha?" Rufus said.

"Please . . ."

"Ain'tcha?"

"Don't hurt my husband."

"We'll be listening for them bedsprings," Rufus told her. "Go ahead, Cherry Boy. Go on in. Enjoy yerself."

Cherry Boy edged toward the room, painfully aware of his "tent."

"Go on, missy."

She followed Cherry Boy into the room.

"And close the door," Rufus added. "You'll want some privacy."

"Don't you wanna watch?" Lucky asked.

"Hell, no, I don't wanna watch," Rufus said, "but I'm gonna go in and get me some when Cherry Boy is finished."

"Hey, Lucky," Sam Sampson said, "that feller's turned all blue."

Lucky looked down at the man beneath his boot and saw that Sampson was right.

"Damn!" he said, pulling his foot off the man's neck.

"Hell," Rufus said, "that feller's plumb dead."

In the other room Cherry Boy and the woman stood awkwardly looking at each other.

"You gotta take your dress off," he said.

"Please," she said, "can you help me?"

"You gotta get undressed."

Hesitantly she started to unbutton her dress.

"Wait," he said, "me first."

He was afraid watching her undress might make him finish faster, so he gingerly pulled his pants down over his hips, holding them away so they wouldn't brush against him. He got them to his ankles and then sat on her big bed to remove his boots, and then his pants. After that he took off his shirt, and finally his underwear. His erection, long and hard and more veined than her husband's, shocked the woman with its size.

"Now you," he said.

She undressed slowly, and he didn't complain. As she peeled away layers of clothing from her skin, he got more and more excited. When she was naked he thought she was the most beautiful thing he'd ever seen. Her breasts were large and round, with thick nipples and tiny blue veins showing beneath the pale skin. Her hips were wide, her thighs a bit chunky. She stood holding her hands down

between her legs, hiding herself. She had never been naked
with a man other than her husband before.

"Move your hands," he said. "I want to look at you."

She moved first one hand, then the other, and he saw the
tangle of black hair between her legs.

"You're beautiful."

She didn't say anything.

"Ain't it proper to thank somebody when they compli-
ment you?" he asked.

"Thank you."

Slowly, Cherry Boy was starting to realize that he was
in charge here. What he said was law and that made him
feel awful powerful.

"Get on the bed."

"Mister—"

"Get on the bed, I said!"

She moved to the bed.

"On your back."

From force of habit she lowered the bedclothes and got
into the bed. She lay rigidly on her back.

Cherry Boy approached the bed and knelt next to it. He
wanted to get a good look at her. He studied her breasts
for some time, then reached out and touched them. First he
ran his fingertips over them, enjoying the warm, smooth
skin, and then he shifted his attention to her nipples, which
puckered when he touched them.

"I ain't all that sure what to do," he said.

"Do—do you want me to tell you?" she asked. She
wanted to get this over with as soon as possible. Sex with
her husband had never been particularly pleasurable for her,
so she couldn't imagine that sex with this stranger would
be anything less than horrible.

"Yeah," he said, "You tell me what to do."

"Get on top of me," she said.

He got on the bed and slid over her. When his skin
touched hers she cringed for a moment, but he was young

and had a good body. It wasn't as horrible as she thought, his skin against hers.

"Now you got to put it in me."

"I know that!" he said. "I ain't dumb . . . but how?"

"Here," she said, and reached down between them to take hold of his penis. In spite of her situation she couldn't help compare him to her husband. This man—this young boy—had a penis that more than filled her hand, unlike her husband's small one. And while it was more veined than her husband's, it felt smoother, almost as if it were made of glass.

And the head was spongy and huge as she pressed it against her. He was big, maybe too big for her—certainly while she was this dry.

"Whatsamatter?" he asked.

"I'm too dry. . . ."

"How do we make you wet?"

"Well . . ."

"Never mind," he said, "I'll just push harder!"

"Wait—"

But he didn't wait. He pushed into her and the dryness of her and the size of him made her cry out in pain. This excited him even more and he continued to pound in and out of her for some time. . . .

"You killed that poor dirt farmer," Rufus said to Lucky.

Lucky looked down at the man's body, then looked at Rufus. "Sorry."

"Ah, forget it," Rufus said. "If he was alive he'd just be goin' crazy listening to how much his wife is enjoying Cherry Boy."

They all heard the cries of the woman from the other room; as a result, they were all getting exited.

Maybe, Sam Sampson thought, she wouldn't be so bad, after all. . . .

•　•　•

Rufus King went into the room with the woman next, and then the others all took their turns. By the time they were done, the sheets were a bloody mess, and the woman was limp and semiconscious.

"Now what?" Cherry Boy asked, as Louis Davis came out of the room, buttoning his trousers.

"Well," Rufus said, "if Lucky hadn't already accidently killed the dirt farmer I'd have you kill him, but I guess you'll have to lose that cherry another way."

"How?"

"You got two choices," Rufus explained. "We can't leave no witnesses behind. You can either kill the woman or the kids."

"Kill 'em? How?"

"With your gun," Rufus said. "That's why you carry one, ain't it? To use it?"

"Yeah, but on a woman and her kids?"

"Hey, it's got to be done, and you get your choice." He pointed. "Door number one or door number two?"

ONE

When Clint Adams rode into Muskogee he wasn't a happy man. First of all, he was doing a job he didn't want to do, and second, he was delivering bad news to a friend.

But he had no one to blame but himself. This was what he got for riding within even a day of Fort Smith. He should have known that a man like Judge Isaac Parker would hear about it. . . .

"Glad you could make it, Adams," the judge had said when Clint entered his office several days earlier.

"Didn't know I had a choice, Judge."

"No, no," Parker said, "everyone has a choice, Mr. Adams."

Yep, Clint thought, you could either befriend Judge Isaac Parker or have him for an enemy.

"What can I do for you, Judge?"

"Well, when I heard you were only a day's ride from here I knew you were the man for the job."

"I'm not wearing a badge," Clint pointed out.

"I remember the last time you agreed to help me with, uh, that Bass Reaves thing, you wouldn't wear a badge. I had one of my men ride with you, though, which sort of gave you official status—if you stretch the point. This time, however, I have no one to send with you.''

"I'm not wearing one of your deputy's badges," Clint said, firmly.

"Why don't we compromise?" Parker asked. He opened his drawer and took out a badge. It was slightly tarnished and had a big dent in the center that had undoubtedly been made by a bullet. It had been a lucky man who had been wearing it that day—maybe.

"Just put it in your pocket," Parker said.

Clint left it where it was.

"Why don't you tell me what this little favor is you want this time, Judge?"

"Well," Parker said, "it ain't so little."

He had not bothered to rise from behind his desk, but Clint could see he'd lost none of his commanding presence since they'd last seen each other.

"Seems there's these five men—well, boys, really, nineteen if they're a day—well, they just seem to be riding around between here and Muskogee just raising all kinds of ruckus this past week or so."

"What kind of ruckus?"

"The rape and murder kind."

"Five nineteen year olds?"

"That's right."

"I hadn't heard about that."

"Well, they're doing it," Parker said. "Killed a family not far from Muskogee, raped the woman, choked the husband to death, and then . . .''

"And then what?"

"Killed the woman and her two kids, too—small children."

"How?"

"Shot them."

"The woman *and* the children?"

"That's right."

"Nineteen year olds?"

"Billy the Kid wasn't much older than that, I seem to recall," Parker said. "And this wasn't the first case, just the worst. Before this they committed a few rapes, even killed some men, but this was the first murder of a woman and her children. These . . . young men have to be stopped, Clint."

"So, send someone to stop them. Send Bass. Or that fellow Murdoch you're so all-fired proud of."

"Can't send either one of them," Parker said. "They're busy. Fact is, there's a hell of a lot of shenanigans going on hereabouts, and I'm just short of men. That's why I was glad to see that piece in that newspaper about you being in Updike."

Updike was a small town a day's ride from Fort Smith. Clint didn't even know the town had a paper, let alone that they had written about him being there. Just another reason to hate journalists, even the small-town kind.

"Judge, I'd like to help you, but—"

"It wouldn't only be me you were helping, Mr. Adams."

"I know," Clint said, "I'd be helping the public, keeping somebody else from being killed. . . ." Parker was not above appealing to a man's civic duty to get him to do what he wanted—or, failing that, blackmail.

"It goes closer to home than that for you."

"Why?"

"One of the boys is young Scott Borton."

Clint was brought up short by that.

"Dave Borton's son?"

"The same. Borton's a friend of yours, isn't he?"

"Yes, he is."

"I thought this might interest you for that reason," Parker said.

"Are you sure Scott's involved?"

"We have a positive indentification from two witnesses who know him on sight. He's with them."

"Damn," Clint said. "I haven't seen Scott since he was eight or nine, I guess."

"A lot can happen to a boy in ten or eleven years, Mr. Adams."

"You know the names of these desperadoes?"

"One of them might be Rufus King," Parker said. "Don't have any word on the others. King would be the brains, though."

"Dave still lives in Muskogee, right?"

"Still there."

Clint thought a minute.

"What about it?" Parker pressed. "Will you help me? Somebody's got to stop these boys and bring them to justice."

Clint knew what "Hanging" Judge Parker meant by justice.

"I'll go to Muskogee and talk to Dave," Clint said. "I'll make my final decision after that."

"Fair enough."

This time Parker did rise and shake hands. When Clint reclaimed his hand, the dented, tarnished star was nestled in it.

"Don't forget that," Parker said.

Clint had hesitated, then put the star in his pocket.

The badge was still in his shirt pocket as he rode into Muskogee. He'd thought about it all the way from Fort Smith, about bringing Scott Borton back with the others, all to have their necks stretched by Judge Parker.

Before he made a final decision he had to talk to Dave Borton.

TWO

Dave Borton had a house outside of town, but the most direct route to it took Clint through town. He figured, since it was late in the day, he might as well get himself a hotel room before continuing on to see him.

Clint left Duke in front of the hotel while he checked in. When he came out there was a man with a badge eyeing the big black gelding.

"Thought I recognized the animal," the sheriff said.

Clint stared at him.

"You don't remember me, do you?" the lawman asked.

Clint studied the man's face. He was young, barely thirty, tall and well built, but, no, he didn't remember him at all.

"I used to be the deputy here," the man said. "Now I'm the sheriff. My name's Terry, Anthony Terry."

"Tony Terry?"

The sheriff grimaced and said, "That's why I use Anthony."

"Whatever you say, Sheriff," Clint said.

"Passing through?"

"Came to see a friend."

13

"Who would that be?"

"Dave Borton."

Terry nodded. "This about his son?"

"Why?"

"If he's hidin' the boy he's lookin' for trouble. Tell him that for me."

"I'll tell him."

The lawman nodded, then looked at Duke and said, "Fine-lookin' animal."

"He's getting a little long in the tooth, like most of us."

"I wouldn't know about that," Terry said, and turned and walked away.

Sure, Clint thought, rub it in.

He mounted Duke and rode out of town, toward Dave Borton's house.

When Clint came within sight of the house, he reined in. Would Borton hide Scott and, by the same virtue, the other members of this gang of nineteen year olds? He looked around but didn't see signs of any other horses. He decided to ride up to the house and see what happened.

He was almost to the door when Dave Borton came out holding a shotgun.

"I told you people to stay away!" he shouted.

"Dave! Hold up! It's me, Clint Adams."

"Clint?" The man squinted at him. Borton had aged since Clint last saw him, but there was no way of knowing if it was an accumulation of years or simply the past week or so with his son.

"By God, it is you," Borton said, putting up the shotgun. "Climb down offa there."

Clint dismounted, dropped Duke's reins to the ground, and approached the house. Borton put out his hand and the two men shook. There was a sour smell to the man, like he'd been sweating a long time and hadn't bathed. It smelled like . . . fear.

"Come on in," Borton said. "I got some corn whiskey I can offer you."

"Sounds good."

They went inside, and Clint was shocked at the disarray of the house. Borton's wife had died years before, but the last time Clint had been there Dave and Scott had kept a neat house. That was not the case now. There were dirty clothes and dirty dishes everywhere.

"You gotta excuse the way the place looks," Borton said. "Since Scott's been gone—you know about that?"

"I heard."

"Since he's been gone I ain't had the heart to straighten up."

He cleared a place at the table for Clint to sit, then found two tin cups and poured some of the whiskey into them from a jug. Clint noticed how the whites of Borton's eyes were shot with red.

"Been drinking a lot of this stuff, Dave?"

"Yeah, I have," Borton admitted, sheepishly. "What brings you here at this time, Clint? Not a good time in my life, as you can see."

"Dave . . . Judge Parker asked me to come and talk to you."

Borton's eyes narrowed.

"You gonna help Parker string up my kid?"

"That's not my intention."

"What is, then?"

"To help, if I can."

"Help who?"

"You. Maybe Scott. Why don't you tell me what's going on, Dave? What's Scott doing running with this kind of crowd?"

"I don't know," Borton said, rubbing his hands over his face. The skin of his hands sounded dry against the stubble of his face. "He's always been a good kid, Clint. You know that."

"I do know."

"Lately ... I don't know, he's been restless. He met these boys in town, fell in with them. ..." Borton shrugged helplessly.

"Has he been around, Dave?"

"No."

"I met the sheriff in town."

"Terry."

"He thinks you might be hiding Scott out here. Wanted me to warn you it wasn't a good idea."

"I'd hide him if he was here," Borton admitted, "but not those others. Not that scum."

Clint believed him. For one thing, there was no way the man could have faked the anguish that was on his face. He'd raised that boy alone, never expecting that something like this would happen.

"When did you last see Scott?"

"Weeks ago," Borton said. "I haven't seen him or heard from him since the first ... incident."

"The first incident?"

"The Bishop family," Borton said. "They choked Ben Bishop to death, raped his wife, and then shot her and the two kids."

This was the story Parker had told him, without the names.

"You think Scott is capable of that, Dave?"

"God," Borton said, burying his face in his hands, "I don't want to, Clint."

But he wasn't sure. He didn't say it, but Clint heard him loud and clear.

Borton looked at Clint. "He's different from when you last saw him. Moody, angry for some reason."

"With you?"

"With the world."

"Do you know why?"

"How can I know why a nineteen-year-old is angry? Maybe because he grew up without a mother."

"You did a fine job, Dave."

"I thought I was doing a good job," Borton said. "I mean, we were friends, we hunted and fished together, worked together—and then he met Rufus King and the others."

That was the second time Clint had heard that name, Rufus King.

"Do you know the names of the others?"

"No," Borton said, "I never wanted to know."

"Tell me about King."

"What's to tell?" Borton asked. "He's got those boys under his power, somehow. He did it to Scott and to those other three. They'll do whatever he says."

"Is he from around here? Is there a father or a mother I could talk to?"

"His mother," Borton said. "She lives a few miles from here. She don't talk to people, though."

"Maybe she'll talk to me. Where does she live, exactly?"

Borton gave Clint directions. Clint stood up to leave and the two men shook hands, but Borton held on to his hand tightly.

"Find my boy, Clint," he said. "Bring him back to me."

"I'll try, Dave."

As he rode away, he realized that the only trouble with keeping his word was that in bringing the boy back to Dave Borton, he would probably also be bringing him back to hang.

THREE

It was getting late in the day, but there was still enough light for Clint to follow Dave Borton's directions to Rufus King's mother's house. From there he'd be able to find his way back to town even in the dark.

The King house was a more run-down version of Dave Borton's two-room wooden home. Clint knew that Borton was proud of that house, having built it himself. That was why it was even more shocking to find that Borton's living conditions had become so slovenly.

As he approached the King house he was greeted in much the same way as he'd been greeted by Dave Borton, but with a rifle this time, not a shotgun, in the hands of an angular woman. That was the only way Clint could think to describe her. She seemed to be all points and angles, a thin woman with bony shoulders, pointy elbows, an angular jaw. She looked to be about five foot seven, and she was a good thirty pounds underweight.

But the rifle she was holding in her hands was rock steady as she pointed it at him.

"Who are ya and whataya want?" she demanded.

"Mrs. King?"

"That's right."

"Is your husband home?"

"That deadbeat's been gone over a dozen years," she said. "If he ever comes back I'll blow his head off without a warning. You, I'm givin' a warning. Get to the point before I pull this trigger. Are you here about my boy?"

"Well, yes, ma'am, I am—"

"Another one, huh?"

"Another what?"

"Another damn bounty hunter," she said. "Well, I'll tell you what I tol' those others. If I knew where Rufus was I'd turn him in myself for the bounty."

"I'm not a bounty hunter, ma'am."

"Who are ya, then?"

He took the badge from his pocket and showed it to her.

"I'm from Judge Parker's court."

"A marshal?"

He didn't answer.

"Well, why didn't ya say so?" she demanded, lowering the rifle. "I got a pot of coffee on, Marshal. Come in and set a spell."

Clint decided to let her continue to call him "Marshal" if it made her more talkative. He dismounted, grounded Duke's reins again, and walked to the house. Up close he could see that the woman was probably not even forty yet. If she put on that missing thirty pounds she might even have been attractive, in a—well, an *angular* sort of way.

"Have a seat at the table, Marshal," she invited, hanging the rifle on two hooks in the wall by the door. "Woman alone can't be too careful, these days, especially with what Rufus and his crew have been up to."

Her hair was pinned behind her head, more gray than black despite her age, and he had the feeling if she unpinned it, it would fall to her waist. In spite of her almost emaciated appearance, she had smooth, pretty skin. Clint wondered if being the mother of Rufus King had anything to do with her appearance.

The house was clean and neat, the way he had remembered Dave Borton's.

She brought a cup of coffee to the table and said, "I got a fresh peach pie I jest took out of the oven not half an hour ago."

He thought he'd smelled something in the air, but had put it down to his imagination, since peach pie was his favorite.

"I'd love a slice."

"I'll get it fer ya," she said. She hurried away and hurried back with it.

"Been a long time since I been able to serve coffee and pie to a man," she said, and then touched her hair.

Clint thought, *Uh oh. If she leaves the room to go fix her hair, I'm in trouble.*

"I'll just be a minute, Marshal. You enjoy your pie."

She left the room, and he knew he was in trouble. This was a lonely woman, and he might be lucky to escape from the house with his virtue intact—so to speak.

When she returned she had indeed fixed her hair, and she had changed her dress, although Clint was hard put to see what this cotton dress had over the other one. It was blue instead of gray, but otherwise identical. She'd also doused herself with some kind of perfume and was smiling, showing teeth that had not been real well taken care of over the years.

She sat opposite him and asked, "Now, what can I do fer you, Marshal?"

"Well—this is very good pie, by the way."

"I'm glad you like it."

"Well, like I was about to say, I was—"

"Some more coffee, Marshal?"

"Well, sure, it's real good, too." It wasn't, but that was beside the point.

He waited while she poured him another cup, returned the pot to the stove, and sat opposite him again, hands folded primly in her lap.

"Like I was saying," he continued, "I was over at Dave Borton's house—"

"Did Judge Parker send you to bring my boy, Dave's boy, and those others to justice?"

"Yes, ma'am, he did."

"I think what they done is an awful thing, Marshal," she said, "awful."

"I agree, Mrs. King."

"Alma," she said, "My name's Alma."

"Alma . . . Was that the truth, what you told me earlier when you thought I was a bounty hunter?"

"God's honest truth, Marshal. I don't hold with what Rufus has been doin', and if I could stop him I would, believe you me."

"I do believe you, Mrs. King. Tell me, can you think of anywhere that Rufus and the others might be hiding?"

"That boy knows the terrain between here and Fort Smith like the back of his hand, Marshal, and he's been to the territories. If he's hidin' he's gonna be hard as hell to find."

Clint frowned.

"But there is this girl . . ."

"What girl?"

"A gal he's sweet on," she said. "She lives over to Carlyle way."

Carlyle was a small town between Muskogee and Fort Smith, almost straddling the border.

"What's the girl's name, Mrs.—Alma?"

"Jenny . . . Jenny somethin'." She frowned. "Cain't recall her last name right now."

"Try, please."

"Well," she said, "if you was to stay to supper I might be able to remember."

"Alma—"

"Woman gets awful lonely for somebody to talk to sometimes," she went on. "And it's gettin' late. After supper you could bed down here and—"

He tried a different tactic. He reached out and took her hand, and she stopped short, her breath catching.

"Alma, as appealing as that is, I really do have to get back to town tonight," he said. "But maybe, if the invitation still stands I could . . . come back when I wasn't working?"

She put her other hand to her chest and said, "Oh my . . . Well, of course the invitation still stands, you silly man."

"Good," he said, patting her hand and then taking his away. "Good. I wouldn't want to . . . miss an opportunity just because I was working."

"I understand," she said, "I truly do, Marshal. You can come back here anytime, just anytime at all."

"Good," he said again, "that's real good."

"Another piece of pie?" she asked.

"No, I really have to be going, Alma," he said, standing, "but there is one thing you could do for me."

"Anything." She also got to her feet. "What is it?"

"Well," he said, "if you could remember that girl's name . . ."

FOUR

Jenny Morse was the girl's name. Apparently she worked in a saloon in Carlyle, Oklahoma. It was dark when Clint left the King house—escaping from the clutches of the lonely Alma King and vowing never to come within fifty miles of the house again. He found his way back to Muskogee easily enough and left Duke in the care of the liveryman. From there he went in search of a meal. Alma's pie had been fine, but her coffee seemed to be burning a hole in his stomach. He needed some food to soak it up, and then some *good* coffee.

He found a small café that was still open and ordered a beef stew that did the trick. While it wasn't delicious, it was edible and soaked up the traces of Alma's coffee nicely. After that he ordered a pot of coffee.

"A whole pot?" the waiter asked.

"I'm expecting company," Clint said, rather than try to justify how much he liked coffee.

The coffee was actually very good; when Clint finished the pot and paid his check, the waiter came over and asked, "Company never showed up, huh?"

"Guess they got busy," Clint said, and left.

His next stop before turning in after a long day was the nearest saloon. When he got there, there was some kind of argument going on at one of the tables. He walked to the bar and got the bartender's attention to order a beer.

"What's it about?" he asked the bartender.

"One of them fellas is a friend of Rufus King," the bartender said.

"Is that a fact?"

"Yeah, and he's tryin' to defend the stealin' and rapin' and killin' that Rufus and his boys are doin'. Folks round here don't like that."

"Maybe this fella's just trying to get some attention for himself."

"Maybe," the bartender said, "but fact is I've seen him in this very saloon with Rufus King on occasion."

"That's interesting."

"You don't know what you're talkin' about," Rufus King's friend was saying. "Rufus is the smartest man I know."

"Man?" someone else said. "He's a boy, barely nineteen, and he's an animal to boot. Animals ain't smart, Freddie; they kill by instinct."

"Rufus ain't no animal," Freddie said. Clint noticed that this fellow was barely nineteen himself. He wondered if Freddie wasn't just a little upset over being left out of Rufus's gang.

The argument went a little longer, and then the crowd really started to turn on Freddie. He decided to leave.

"You'll see!" he shouted from the door. "You'll all see!"

He left without telling them *what* they'd see.

"Thanks," Clint said to the bartender, and followed Freddie outside.

"Hey!" he called out.

Freddie turned and seemed ready to grab his gun.

"Take it easy," Clint said. "I just want to talk."

"About what?" Freddie asked, narrowing his eyes suspiciously.

"I know you, don't I?"

"I don't think I know you."

"You're Freddie ... wait a minute, don't tell me ... Freddie ..."

"Gruber."

"Yeah, that's right," Clint said. "Gruber. You're friends with Rufus King."

Freddie's face brightened.

"That's right!"

"I think they were pretty unfair to you, in there," Clint said.

"Yeah, they was."

"They probably don't know what good friends you and Rufus are."

"Yeah."

"Or maybe they're just jealous."

"Yeah, that's it," Freddie said, brightening. "They're jealous."

"You know what?" Clint asked. "I'd like to buy you a drink, but not in that dump. Do you know where there's a good saloon."

"There's another one right up the street."

"Well, come on, then," Clint said. "It'd be my honor to buy a drink for a friend of Rufus King's."

"Hey, thanks, mister," Freddie said, and they headed for the other saloon. "You know, I coulda been a member of that gang...."

FIVE

Freddie truly did feel he had been left out of something good when Rufus didn't put him in his gang.

"I don't understand it," he whined over a third or fourth drink. "We was friends. Why didn't he take me wit' him?"

They were sitting at a secluded table, and it was getting later and later. The gaming tables had been closed down and only one girl was still working the floor. Clint had been hoping that the next drink might pry some piece of information out of Freddie's head, but he was starting to think that Freddie had been left out of Rufus's gang for a reason.

He was a tedious bore.

All he did was cry about how great it would have been to be a part of Rufus's gang and how great Rufus was. Even Rufus, Clint was sure, would have tired of this constant praise.

" 'Nother drink," Freddie said. Then his head hit the table.

"You're lucky, mister," the girl said, stopping by the table.

"Why's that?"

"It usually takes a few more drinks to put Freddie to sleep like that."

"Is he out for the night?" Clint asked.

"Oh, yeah," she said.

Clint looked at her. She appeared to be twenty-five, pretty with a lush body that almost spilled out of her dress when she leaned over to take a closer look at Freddie.

"He's out."

"What should I do with him?"

"Just leave him," she said. "Jess'll take care of him."

"Jess?"

"The bartender," she said. "All the bartenders in town know Freddie."

"Why's that?"

"Because he's chewed all their ears about how he and Rufus King are such great friends."

"And they aren't?"

"Are you kiddin'?" she asked. "If they were, don't you think Freddie would be wherever Rufus is?"

"Do you know Rufus?"

"Me? I seen him a time or two."

"But you wouldn't say you were friends?"

She rolled her eyes.

"Rufus is crazy, mister," she said. "I don't need no crazy kids in my life."

"Kids?"

"Well, he's only nineteen, right? Say, maybe that's why Rufus didn't take Freddie."

"Why?"

"Freddie's twenty."

"Twenty? I thought he was nineteen."

"Turned twenty six months ago, but kept tellin' folks he was nineteen, hoping Rufus'd be friends with him."

"What's your name?"

"Stacy."

"How do you know so much about Freddie?"

She gave the dozing Freddie a look and said, "The stupid sod is my cousin."

"Can't you take him home, then?"

"Jess's his uncle," she said, "and my dad. He'll get him home."

"So Rufus is too young for you?"

"Hell, yes," she said. "I'm twenty-four, and I like more . . . mature men."

Suddenly, the situation had turned flirtatious, which Clint didn't mind.

"Is that a fact?"

"How old are *you*?" she asked.

"Older than twenty-four."

"See?" she said. "You're mature."

"At least."

"Just get into town today?"

"That's right."

"I figured I would have seen you before this," she said. "Stayin' long?"

"Probably leaving tomorrow."

"Shoot, the good ones are always in a hurry to leave."

"Sorry."

"That's okay," she said, then cocked one rounded hip and asked, "Want some company for the night?"

"Um, I don't usually pay for company—"

"That's okay," she said, "I don't usually charge for it. I've had my eye on you all night, but you didn't notice because you were plyin' Freddie with liquor. What were you tryin' to get out of him?"

"Why should I be trying to get something out of him?" he asked.

"Mister," she said, "nobody drinks with my cousin Freddie 'cause they want to. You're lookin' for Rufus, ain't you?"

"What if I was?"

She shrugged.

"No skin off my nose. My offer still stands. Company

for the night, no money, no strings. The men in this town are so boring.''

"I'll try to avoid it," he said.

"Somehow," she said, looking at him closely, "I don't think you'd have to try too hard.''

SIX

He didn't.

She came to his room soon after their conversation and without a word—but with a lascivious look on her pretty face—removed all of her clothes. Her body was full and lush, big round breasts and fleshy hips and butt. He filled his hands with her breasts right away, popping the nipples between his fingers, licking them, nipping at them, sliding his hands over her opulent curves, down between her legs where she was already so wet he could smell her. He slid his middle finger along her oozing cleft, and she moaned and began humping his hand, bumping and grinding with her hips, sucking in her bottom lip, and then *his* bottom lip as they kissed juicily.

He moved her to the bed and pushed her down on it. He started to undress, and she slid her own hand between her legs and chanted, "Hurry, hurry, hurry . . ." He began to realize that this woman didn't just love sex, she *needed* it.

When he was naked she grabbed him and pulled him to her and roamed his body with her hands and mouth until she was sucking him avidly, making sounds liked "yum" and "um" and "oh" as she suckled him wetly. Then she

mounted him hurriedly, took him in both of her hands and
guided him to her, then sat on him, taking him deeply inside. After that, he actually got the feeling that he didn't
have to be there—just his penis did. She rode him up and
down with total abandon, using him to seek her own pleasure, her eyes closed, biting her lips, her head thrown back
so that the cords on her neck stood out. . . .

And then the door flew open from a kick; a man charged
in with a gun in his hand, and Clint knew he'd been set
up. Stacy dove for the floor and Clint reached for his gun,
which was hanging on the bedpost. It was a well-practiced
move, and as bullets thudded into the mattress around him,
he coolly shot the man in the chest. The bullets struck him
with such force that it propelled him out the door and back
into the hall.

Then Clint turned his gun on the girl, who was staring
up at him with wide, unfocused eyes.

"Wait, wait," she said, holding her hands out in front
of her. "He made me, he made me do it, said he'd kill
me . . ."

"Don't move," he told her.

She nodded, still holding her hands out, her eyes so unfocused that he thought she was still in the throes of sexual
passion.

He got off the bed and walked naked into the hall to
check the man. It was Freddie, lying on his back, his gun
on the floor a few feet from him. There were some other
people in the hall, men and women, who stared at his na-
kedness and at the dead man.

"Is he dead?" Stacy asked when he reentered the room.
"Yes."

"Good," she said, "close the door and we can finish.
The bastard's timing was all off."

"What? You want to finish?"

"Look at yourself," she said, her hands moving over her
own body. "You still want me."

He looked down and found that he had lost none of his

hardness. Maybe she was right, maybe he still wanted her body, but there were too many people in the hall for one of them not to have called the sheriff.

"Get dressed," he said, "the law will be here soon."

"The law?"

He grabbed his pants and pulled them on. People were sticking their heads in the room to see what was going on. One man gasped when he saw Stacy naked.

"Get out of here!" Clint shouted, and the man's head withdrew.

She got on the bed and faced him, still nude.

"You're not gonna tell the sheriff—"

"Tell him what? That you set me up to be killed? Now, why wouldn't I tell him that, Stacy?"

"Clint," she said, "Clint, we can go back to what we were doing when the sheriff leaves. I can make you real happy—"

"You were making me real happy, Stacy, but how would I know that some other guy wasn't going to come through the door, or the window, with a gun?"

"There ain't nobody else."

"You're great in bed, Stacy," he said, "but not great enough to die for. Get dressed."

SEVEN

When Sheriff Terry arrived, the first thing he did was force everyone back into their rooms. Then he took a look at the body.

"Freddie Gruber," he said.

"You know him?" Clint asked.

"Sure," Terry said, "big talker. Lately he's been claiming to be Rufus King's friend." Terry looked at Clint. "Why was he after you?"

"I don't know," Clint said, "but there's somebody in my room who might."

They both entered the room. Stacy was sitting on the bed, dressed in her work clothes again, her hands folded demurely in her lap. It was a gesture Clint recalled Alma King using as well.

"Stacy?" Sheriff Terry asked. "What do you know about this?"

"Not much, Sheriff," she said. "All I know is Freddie paid me to come up here with Mr. Adams and, um, keep him busy."

"You didn't know why?"

"No."

"He didn't tell you he was gonna try to kill this man?" the sheriff asked.

"No, sir!"

"She's lying," Clint said. "She hit the floor as soon as the door flew open."

Terry frowned at Stacy.

"Sheriff, I swear," she said, leaning forward to give the lawman a good look at her cleavage.

. "Now, you sit up straight, girl," Terry said. "Don't try none of that stuff with me."

"She told me Freddie was her cousin."

"Cousin!" Terry snorted. "He's her boyfriend—that is, he was."

"He wasn't my boyfriend," she said. "He told people that."

"What was he, then?" Terry asked.

"He just . . . bought me things."

"And slept with you."

"When he had the money."

"Well," Terry said, "he had the money to pay you to sleep with Mr. Adams, didn't he?"

Stacy sighed and both men noticed what it did to her big breasts.

"He said he wanted to help Rufus," she said, finally. "This man was buying him drinks, asking questions about Rufus. When he came to the bar one time he told me he was gonna pretend to pass out, and then I was to come up here with him and keep him busy." She looked up at both of them imploringly. "I swear to you he didn't say nothin' about killing anybody."

"It would have been a good guess, though," Clint said. He looked at the sheriff. "He probably thought killing me would put him in good with Rufus King, and maybe King'd make him part of the gang."

Terry looked at the broken door, and the body on the floor in the hall, then looked at Stacy.

"Well, Stacy, you better come with me."

"What for?"

"I'll have to lock you up."

"Sheriff—" she began, but Clint beat her to it.

"Don't."

"What?"

"Let her go."

"Why? She helped him try to kill you."

"You won't be able to prove that in court," Clint said. "It would be a waste of time."

Terry started to say something, then stopped and looked at the girl again.

"Do you know who this man is?"

She shrugged.

"He said his name was Clint."

"That's right," Sheriff Terry said, "Clint *Adams*."

Her eyes went wide immediately, and she asked, "The Gunsmith?"

"Now you've got it," Terry said. "You're lucky he didn't kill you himself in all the excitement—but he might, if you try anything again."

"Goddamnit!" she said, stamping her foot. "That idiot didn't tell me he was gonna try somethin' with the Gunsmith."

"Well," Terry said, "you're lucky that idiot didn't get you killed, and you're lucky Mr. Adams, here, is ready to let you go."

"You mean . . . I *can* go?"

"Get out of here, Stacy."

He didn't have to tell her twice. She launched herself off the bed, slipped between them, stepped over Freddie's dead body, and was gone.

"I suppose the bartender's not her dad and Freddie's uncle, either."

"Jess? Hell, no."

"Well," Clint said, "at least she got his name right."

"I'll get this body moved," the sheriff said.

"Does Rufus King have any other friends like this in town?"

"Not that I know of," Sheriff Terry said, "but if I was you, I'd keep my eyes open."

"Oh, I will," Clint said, "all night. Tomorrow, I'm out of here."

"Sounds like a good plan," the sheriff said. "A real good plan."

EIGHT

Clint slept the rest of the night with one eye open. It didn't help that the sheets still smelled of Stacy, her perfume, her musk, her excitement. Would it have been so bad to let her stay after the sheriff had gone?

He woke in the morning with a raging erection and could only douse water on his face and chest. He didn't have time for a cold bath.

He had a quick breakfast in the hotel dining room, then walked to the livery—keeping alert every step of the way—to retrieve Duke.

He realized that it wasn't so much that he had to watch out for friends of Rufus King's, but for those who were looking to impress him and get into his gang.

When he came out of the livery with Duke, he found Sheriff Terry waiting for him.

"Making sure I leave?" he asked.

"Making sure you leave safely," Terry said. "I don't want to become known as the sheriff of the town where the Gunsmith was killed."

"You don't have to worry," Clint said, mounting up. "I'm gone."

"Good luck."

When he rode out of Muskogee he had an itch right in the middle of his back.

The ride to Carlyle took a few hours. Between there and Muskogee he kept expecting another attempt on his life, but none came. Now all he had to worry about was somebody in Carlyle making a try for him.

Carlyle was much smaller than Muskogee. He didn't see any telegraph wires, so at least no one could have gotten a telegram about him coming there. All he had to do was be a little discreet in asking his questions.

There were only two saloons in town, so finding a girl named Jenny Morse shouldn't present a big problem. He debated about whether or not to put up Duke in the livery, then decided to go ahead. The town apparently had one hotel, but he couldn't imagine that it would be full. If he needed to get a room later, there should be one available.

After he left the livery, he walked to the first saloon. As he entered he saw that there were no girls. He should have realized that they probably wouldn't start working until later.

He walked to the bar.

"Help ya?" the barman asked.

"Beer."

The man drew the beer and set it in front of Clint.

"First one today," he said. "Nice and cold."

"Thanks."

Clint sipped it and nodded approvingly at the bartender.

"I'm looking for a girl," he said.

"Ain't we all?"

The bartender would be looking a long time, if that was the case. He was ugly, pure and simple. Nose flattened against his face, crooked, thick-lipped mouth, a tooth missing in every other space, it seemed. He was big and hairy. His forearms were covered with wiry black hair, and a tuft of it stuck out of his shirt, as if his whole body were covered with it.

" 'Course," the bartender said, "some of us will be lookin' longer than others."

He knew he was ugly, and he laughed about it.

"I'm looking for one woman in particular," Clint said. "Her name's Jenny Morse."

"Don't know her."

"She's supposed to work in a saloon in this town," Clint said. "At least, that's what my friend told me. Told me to look her up if I ever came to Carlyle."

"Don't know her," the bartender said, again. "Try the other saloon."

"What's it called?"

The bartender shrugged and said, "Only two saloons in town, what's the point of naming them? I just call it the other saloon."

"I'll check over there, then."

As Clint finished his beer the bartender said, "We got better beer than they do."

"Do you have better girls?"

"I doubt it," the man said. "We got no girls here."

"Why not?"

"They cause too much trouble," the barman said. "Fights and stuff."

"I see."

"We don't need no fights in here. Damages the furniture."

Clint looked around at the table and chairs, some of which already looked pretty damaged.

"We got a reputation to look after," the bartender explained.

"Well," Clint said, "you do have good beer, that's for sure."

He paid for the beer and started for the door.

"Hope you find your girl," the bartender called out.

"Thanks."

"Take my advice, though."

"What's that?"

"Wait a few hours before you go lookin'," the man said.
"She'll be easier to find, then."

"I'll keep that in mind," Clint said.

NINE

Clint decided to take the bartender's advice, and that meant getting a room in the hotel. He walked over there and had to wake the dozing clerk to check in.

"Do you have a room?" he asked.

"We got lots of rooms," the clerk said, with a bored expression.

"Available rooms?"

"More than half of them are empty," the clerk said. "That available enough for you?"

There was a short roof out in front of the hotel, so Clint said, "I'd like something off the alley."

"I can give you room with a view of the street," the clerk said.

"The alley will be just fine."

"Suit yourself." The man handed him a key. "Number eight."

"Thanks."

Clint went up to the room to take a look at it. He had left his saddlebags and rifle over at the livery, so that was going to have to be his next stop, to pick them up.

When he got to the room he could see why more than

45

half of them were empty. It smelled musty, as if it hadn't been cleaned in months. The mattress was little better than a pallet in a jail cell.

He walked to the window and looked out. It was a straight drop to the alley. That suited him just fine.

He left the room and headed for the livery.

Walking back from the livery, rifle in his left hand, saddlebags over his left shoulder, he decided to stop in and see the sheriff. When he found the sheriff's office, though, it was boarded up. There was a shingle hanging from one chain that said, in faded letters, SHERIFF PETE SYKES. Obviously, Sheriff Sykes didn't live there anymore.

He went back to the hotel to stow his saddlebags and rifle in his room. The clerk was dozing again, and Clint was careful not to wake him as he went up the steps.

He waited in his room a few hours, then left and headed for the "other" saloon to see if anyone there knew Jenny Morse.

When he entered the other saloon, he found it—unlike the hotel—more than half full. There was plenty of room at the bar so he bellied up and ordered a beer. The bartender at the first saloon was right. They did have better beer than this place, but it was obvious that this place had better furniture, a few games going, and three girls working the floor. If one of them was Jenny Morse it would make his task a whole lot easier.

"Hey, Becky, darlin', how about a beer?" a man called.

A pretty dark-haired girl said, "Comin' up, Ben."

That was when Clint decided that if he just kept quiet, nursed a beer, and kept his ears open, he'd find out if one of the girls was Jenny.

Becky brought Ben a beer, and he slapped her on the rump for it.

A little later somebody called the redhead Colleen and

slapped her on the rump. Both girls had real nice rumps, too.

The third girl had hair like spun gold, skin like alabaster, and—when she passed him—he saw that her eyes were a startling china blue. If this was the Jenny that Rufus King was smitten with, he could see why. She was, however, at first glance a good five or six years older than the young killer.

"Jenny," the bartender called, "take these beers to Cal Bennett's table."

"Right away, Mike," the blonde said, and there he had it. The blonde was Jenny. What were the chances her name was *not* Jenny Morse?

Now Clint had a decision to make. He could talk to the girl, see if she knew Rufus King, and if she knew where he was. If she *was* his girlfriend, she wouldn't admit to knowing him and would warn him as soon as she could that someone was looking for him.

His second course of action was to wait and see if Rufus King came to see her, or if he could hear someone mention him. Waiting for him to come and see her could take days, weeks. He decided to order another beer and see if the conversation ever got around to the band of nineteen-year-old killers.

TEN

After a few hours he was wondering if anyone in that saloon even knew there were five nineteen-year-olds going around killing people.

He decided he was going to have to push it. He ordered another beer and then brought up the subject when the bartender came with it.

"Heard there's been some excitement around here," he said.

"Yeah?" the bartender asked. "Around here, you say?"

"Well . . . near here, anyway."

"Oh, you must mean"—the bartender lowered his voice—"the Rufus King thing."

"Rufus King?"

The man nodded.

"Yeah, he and his boys have been, uh, doin' stuff they shouldn't be doin'."

"Why are we whispering?" Clint asked.

"See that blonde over there?" He was referring to Jenny.

"I see her. I've been watching her all afternoon. Pretty girl."

"Yeah, well, she's Rufus King's girl."

49

"She is?"

The man nodded.

"She don't like to hear nothin' said against Rufus, so nobody around here really talks about it much."

"I see. She must be pretty popular, then."

"Well, she was," the bartender said, "until men around here found out she was Rufus's girl. Now she's like, you know, sort of exclusive."

"Doesn't that cut into your business?" Clint asked.

"Hey," the man said, "I ain't no pimp. What the girls do after hours is their business—but, I tell ya, the other two girls ain't complainin'. They keep pretty busy."

"I guess so."

"You just passin' through?"

"That's right," Clint said. "Just for the night."

"Well, take my advice: Don't talk about Rufus around here."

"He got friends here?"

"Not here," the bartender said. "His only friend around here is Jenny. Nobody else thinks much of him."

"I'll keep that in mind—hey, wait a minute."

"What?"

"Does he actually come here to see her?"

The bartender nodded and replied, "Every week."

"What about the law?"

"Sheriff Sykes gave up on this place a long time ago," the man said, "and the town ain't seen fit to replace him— and that was before Rufus and his gang went on their . . . spree."

"I understand," Clint said. "I guess with no lawman hereabouts it's pretty safe for Rufus King and his gang to come to town, huh?"

"The gang don't come," the barman said, "just Rufus."

Clint looked around, acting as if he were nervous.

"He's not here now, is he?"

"Not that I can see," the bartender said, "but that don't mean he ain't on his way. He's about due."

"Maybe I better finish my beer and go stay in my hotel room," Clint said.

"Nah," the man said, "have another. Rufus don't cause no trouble—that is, unless he sees somebody talkin' to Jenny."

"Just talking to her?"

The barkeep nodded. "He goes kind of crazy, then, and he's pretty good with a gun."

"You don't mean he's already killed somebody for talking to her, do you?"

"Damn near," the man said. "Shot a fella's ear off, right from the door. Walked in and saw him sittin' with Jenny. Just drew and fired. Fella went out the window, minus an ear."

That story had all the *ear*marks of a fairy tale, Clint thought. "She is real pretty, though," he said aloud, watching Jenny move across the room. "Might be worth losing an ear for."

"Maybe," the bartender said, "but not worth gettin' killed for."

"You're probably right."

The bartender moved to the other end of the bar to refill a beer mug, so Clint turned and watched Jenny some more. Was this the same kind of thing as with Stacy in Muskogee? Did Rufus King think that Jenny Morse was his girl? Or was she actually?

She moved easily across the floor, flirting with men at their tables, bringing them drinks. None of the men looked nervous about it, worried that they might lose an ear—or worse.

Was the bartender just building up the Rufus King legend? Maybe business picked up if people thought that Rufus King might show up.

Did King have that kind of reputation in these parts, already.

ELEVEN

It was amazing how quickly Cherry Boy had taken to the raping and the killing. He liked it so much he didn't even mind that Rufus and the others just kept on calling him Cherry Boy. In fact, he sort of liked the name.

The five of them were sitting their horses within sight of a small ranch house.

"This family's got a fifteen-year-old blonde daughter," Rufus said. "She is so young and fresh and sweet."

"What are we waitin' for?" Cherry Boy asked.

"Now, just hold on, Cherry Boy," Rufus said. "Don't be in such an all-fired hurry. There's also a mama, a papa, and some brothers involved."

"We can take care of all of 'em," Cherry Boy said eagerly.

"Maybe we can," Rufus replied, "but we can't just ride up to the house and start shootin'. We got to have a plan."

"What kind of plan?"

"I got to think on it," Rufus said.

"Uh-oh," Sam Sampson said.

The others knew what that meant.

"Rufus is goin' to Carlyle," Lucky Davis said.

53

"To see Jenny," Louis Davis said.

"Who's Jenny?" Cherry Boy asked.

"Rufus's sweetie," Sampson said. "Saloon gal in Carlyle. Prettiest little blonde you'd ever want to see."

"There's a blonde down there," Cherry Boy said, indicating the house. "Blonde and fresh and sweet—you said so yourself, Rufus."

"I got to think, Cherry Boy," Rufus repeated. "The boys and you will hide out while I go to Carlyle."

"Why can't we come with you?" the newest member of the gang asked.

"Because there's lawmen lookin' for us," Rufus said. "They're lookin' for the Rufus King *gang*. We can't go ridin' into a town like a gang, can we?"

"Ain't no law in Carlyle," Sampson reminded him.

"Judge Parker's got to have some deputy marshal out lookin' for us by now," Rufus said. "I ain't worried about no town sheriff. What if we ride into Carlyle and Parker's man is there?"

"We kill him." Cherry Boy said.

Rufus King laughed.

"Listen to Cherry Boy now," he said. "He wants to kill one of Judge Parker's men."

"That'd bring a whole passel of trouble down on us," Lucky Davis said.

"Killin's killin'." Cherry Boy shrugged.

"Spoken like a real expert," Rufus said, and then added, "But you ain't, son, so you'll do as you're told. Understand?"

"Sure, Rufus, sure," Cherry Boy said, "I understand."

And he thought, *But I don't have to like it.*

TWELVE

Well, if any part of what the bartender said was correct, maybe Rufus King *was* due in Carlyle any time. If his visits were weekly, it should only take a few days to determine whether or not he was going to skip a week.

Clint took advantage of the remaining daylight to take a look around Carlyle. There wasn't much to it, just a few stores, a church, the hotel, the two saloons, and a few houses around it. Everybody seemed to know everybody, so he drew looks everywhere he went as a stranger in town.

He decided to go to the livery on the pretense of checking on Duke, engage the liveryman in conversation. He'd found in the past that after bartenders, liverymen were the people who saw and heard the most.

"Back so soon?" the man asked.

"Just wanted to check my horse's right foreleg," Clint said. "He might have been favoring it a bit."

"Seemed okay to me," the man said, "but let's take a look."

They walked back to Duke's stall together. The livery-man was small in stature, standing barely five five, but Clint could see the muscles bunching in his arms as he lifted the big gelding's foreleg.

"Seems okay to me," he said again. "You want to take a look?"

"No, that's okay," Clint said. "You seem to know what you're doing, and you have a pretty good touch. If you didn't he would have taken your head off by now."

"Naw," the man said, patting Duke's massive neck once, "me and this big boy is gettin' along okay."

Clint knew that Duke didn't take to many people, but when he ran into a man who knew horses the big gelding managed to get along.

"This is quite an animal," the man said. "I never seen one like him."

"Neither have I." He stuck his hand out and said, "My name's Clint."

"Jerry Bailey," the other man replied. His handshake was firm. "I know who you are."

"You do?"

The man nodded.

"Heard tell about this big gelding of yours. Never thought I'd get to see him, though. What brings you to town?"

"A girl."

"What girl would that be?"

"Jenny Morse."

"Oh," Bailey said, "the blonde one over to the saloon."

"That's her."

Bailey had a wizened little face, and could have been anywhere from forty to sixty. His eyes twinkled now, though, talking about the blonde.

"Gotta watch out for her."

"Why's that?"

"Rufus King's got an eye for her."

"I heard she was his girl."

Bailey laughed and said, "Not hardly. You heard that from the bartender, Jake, didn't ya?"

"I did, yeah," Clint said, "but he didn't tell me his name."

"Yeah, it's Jake. He owns the place. He's been tellin' stories like that ever since Rufus got famous. He tell you about Rufus shootin' off a feller's ear?"

"Yep, he told me that one, too."

"That never happened, neither. Naw, Rufus is sweet on Jenny, but she don't want nothin' to do with him. Fact is, she don't want nothin' to do with any man from Carlyle or hereabouts." Bailey's eyes narrowed. "Why you lookin' fer her?"

"A friend of mine told me about her," Clint said. "Told me if I was anywhere near this town I should stop in and take a look."

Bailey backed up a step or two and studied Clint for a minute.

"That's got about as much ring of truth to it as one of Jake's stories," he said finally.

"No, really, I—"

Bailey held up his hand to stop Clint. It was gnarled and scarred, the way a man's hand gets when he's around the flashing, gnashing teeth of horses his whole life.

"You don't have to try to explain it," he said. "Whatever yer doin' here it's yer own business. My money's on Rufus, though."

"How do you mean?"

"This is a no-account town. I'd bet yer here because of him—though I never did hear of you hunting bounty."

"I don't."

"I do hear tell you like to do favors for friends, though," Bailey said.

Clint frowned. With all the stories that circulated about him, he didn't know about that one. He did do favors for friends, but didn't know that other people knew it.

"Maybe Rufus did some harm to a friend of yours and you're out to get him—no, no, you don't have to tell me nothin'."

"I wouldn't want you spreading that around, Jerry."

"You don't got to threaten me none, either. I ain't gonna say nothin'."

"I wasn't threatening you."

"Don't matter," Bailey said. "My lips is sealed. You go on about yer business, and I'll look after the big boy, here."

"That's a deal," Clint said.

THIRTEEN

The first problem with waiting in a town for someone to show up was that they might not show up. The second problem was finding something to do while you waited. In a decent-size town, Clint was sure he'd be able to scare up a poker game to while away the time. In a town like Carlyle, he wasn't so sure. Maybe he'd be able to find somebody who'd want to play horseshoes.

Walking the town had shown him one thing. The two saloons were within sight of each other. He had a choice of taking a table in the same saloon where Jenny worked, or watching that saloon from the one across the street. In a town this size he had already been noticed as a stranger. Also, he couldn't really depend on Bailey, the liveryman, keeping his word and not telling anyone who he was. He decided the best thing to do was just take up a position in the saloon where the girl worked and see what happened.

When something did happen, it happened soon.

It was the next day, and he was sitting at a back table watching Jenny work the floor with the other girls. Suddenly, she came over to his table.

"Another one?"

"Not yet. I can still—"

"Have another one and we can talk," she said, quickly and quietly.

"Well, okay," he said, "I'll have another."

She got him a fresh beer from the bar and carried it to his table, then sat down.

"Aren't you afraid somebody will see you sitting there?" he asked.

"It's part of the job, to talk to the customers," she said. "That's what I'm doing. Talking."

"What do you want to talk about?"

"You. What do you want?"

"What makes you think I want something?"

"You've been watching me since you got here yesterday."

"Don't men usually watch you?"

"All the time," she said, "but not the way you are."

"And how am I watching?"

"Like a hawk."

"Look, Jenny—"

"Is this about Rufus King? Is that what this is about?" she demanded.

"Jenny, I—"

"Goddamn him for spreading the word that I'm his girl. I'm not. I'm not interested in that little shit. He's too young, he's too ugly, and he's too much trouble."

"Have you told him that?"

She backed off a bit.

"He'd kill me."

"So you tolerate him?"

"I bring him beer and sit with him."

"You don't . . ."

"No," she said firmly, "I don't."

"Doesn't he press you for it?"

"Yes, but for some reason he . . . he treats me different than other women."

"You mean he doesn't rape you."

She bit her lip.

"Does he sleep with the other girls?"

"No," she said, "he's waiting for me to sleep with him without him paying me."

Clint grimaced as he realized that he and the young killer had that in common.

"Is that going to happen?"

"I hope not," she said. "Not if I can get out of this town."

"How do you intend to do that?"

"I'm saving my money."

"Did you ever think of collecting the bounty on him?"

"He'd kill me if I tried," she said. She looked around nervously. "I have to go back to work. If you are waiting for Rufus King, will you promise me something?"

"What?"

She stood up.

"When he gets here, would you kill him, please?"

FOURTEEN

Jenny's request might have been on the level. Clint didn't make any promises to her as she walked away. He looked around to see if anyone had been paying any particular attention to them. If they had been, they were doing it discreetly.

He'd heard the same story from Stacy in Muskogee and now from Jenny in Carlyle. Rufus King thought they were his girls, acted like they were his girls, but they couldn't stand him. Apparently, they were too afraid of him to tell him so.

Clint couldn't wait to get a look at this nineteen-year-old desperado who had everybody so scared.

Rufus King halted his horse just outside of Carlyle and turned in his saddle to regard the members of his gang.

"You boys know where to meet me, right?"

"Right," Lucky Davis said.

"And when?"

"Three days," Sam Sampson said.

"Don't leave until I get there, understand?" he asked.

"We understand, Rufus," Louis Davis said.

Rufus turned his eyes on Cherry Boy, who had changed quite a bit since his first kill.

"Do you understand, Cherry Boy?"

"Sure, Rufus," he answered, "I understand real good."

"Make sure you do."

Rufus turned and rode on toward Carlyle.

"What's Carlyle like?" Cherry Boy asked.

"It's a hole," Lucky said.

"Nothin' there," Sampson said.

"A dead town," Louis said.

"Except for this gal, Jenny, right?" Cherry Boy asked.

"Right," Louis said.

"She must be real good-lookin'," Cherry Boy mused.

"Get it out of your mind, Cherry Boy," Sam Sampson said. "In this gang, you do what Rufus says or he'll kill ya."

"Yeah," Cherry Boy said, "so I hear, only I ain't seen him kill anybody yet."

"What?" Sampson asked.

"Lucky, you killed that dirt farmer, crushed his throat."

"I tole you that was an accident."

"I did the two brats," Cherry Boy said, "and Lucky did the woman. That family after that? It was me and Louis did the killin'."

"So?" Sampson asked. "What's your point?"

"Only that I ain't seen the big killer kill nobody yet."

"Don't worry," Sampson said, "Rufus's killed plenty of people. Plenty."

"You see him do any?" Cherry Boy demanded.

"Well, no . . ." Sampson admitted, ". . . but he *said*—"

"How about you boys?" he asked the others. "Anybody see Rufus kill anybody?"

The Davis brothers exchanged nervous glances, then looked at Sampson, who said, "Come on, this ain't gettin' us nowhere. We got to go to the hideout."

"Sure," Cherry Boy said, "because that's what Rufus said we got to do."

"Right," Sampson said.

"Well, go ahead, then, Sam," Cherry Boy said. "Lead the way."

FIFTEEN

The first few hours in his room that night were fitful for Clint. He didn't need to have anybody else come bursting in on him. He took the pitcher from the dresser and set it on the windowsill so that anybody trying to get in that way would knock it over. After that he took the chair from the corner and jammed it underneath the doorknob.

He hung his gunbelt on the bedpost and removed his shirt and boots, but kept his trousers on.

Nineteen-year-olds who liked to kill. Whatever happened to chasing girls, or riding and roping, or even drinking to blow off steam? Raping and killing? The world was going to hell—you only had to look at the anguished face of Dave Borton to know that.

Clint felt sorry for his friend. He was here at the behest of Judge Parker, but even if Rufus King walked up to him and gave himself up, it was Scott Borton whom he was going to keep looking for.

He was just drifting off to sleep when there was a knock at his door. He came awake with a start and grabbed his gun from the holster.

"Who is it?" he asked at the door.

"Jenny Morse," she said. "Let me in before somebody sees me."

He unlocked the door and opened it only wide enough to make sure no one was with her. He'd already been burned by Stacy in Muskogee.

"Are you gonna let me in?"

He backed up, let her enter, and closed the door.

"What are you doing here?"

"I thought we had to talk."

"We did talk."

"I thought we had to talk more."

She was wearing a shawl over her dress. She removed it and dropped it on the bed. Her pale cleavage was even more alluring in a hotel room than it had been in the saloon.

"Can you put that away?" she asked, indicating the gun. "It makes me nervous."

"I'm sorry," Clint said. "The last time a woman came to my room, a man kicked in the door and tried to shoot me."

"Jealous husband?" she asked.

"Someone who thought he was a friend of Rufus King," Clint said. "He was trying to do King a favor."

"And you got him?"

"That's why I'm still here."

He walked to the bedpost and holstered the gun.

"You never answered me."

"When?"

"When I asked you if you'd kill Rufus King and get him out of my life."

"I guess that's going to be his choice."

"He's a boy and you're a man," she said. "It shouldn't be too hard."

"From what I hear he's a pretty dangerous boy, surrounded by other dangerous boys."

"Why are you after him?"

He walked to his shirt and took the badge from his pocket.

"This is one reason."

"You're a deputy marshal?" Her eyes widened.

"Actually," he said, "I was never properly sworn in. I'm doing this as a favor to Judge Parker."

"But that ain't the only reason?"

"No," he said. "I have a friend whose nineteen-year-old son has apparently fallen under Rufus King's spell. I'm going to try to get him back."

"What if he's already raped and killed along with Rufus?" she asked.

"I'll have to bring him back, one way or another."

"You mean dead or alive?"

"I mean whether he's killed someone or not."

She sat on the bed, picked up the shawl, and started playing with it.

"What's going on, Jenny?" Clint asked. "Why are you nervous?"

"Because I'm afraid if you don't get Rufus he'll get me."

"I'll get him," Clint said, "don't worry about that. Do you know something that might help me?"

"Well," she said, "when he comes to town he comes alone."

"And where does he leave his gang?"

She waved, using the hand that held the shawl, so that the garment lashed out and back like a whip.

"Out there. They've got a hideout somewhere."

"You don't know where it is?"

"Now, how would I know that?" she asked. "I ain't Rufus King's girl. He don't talk to me about stuff like that."

"All right, all right," he said. "I believe you—but something is making you awful nervous. What is it?"

She looked up at him, those china blue eyes wide and imploring.

"You won't miss?"

"I won't."

"You'll take him in?"

"I will."

"And if he resists, and shoots at you, you'll kill him?"

"I'll do what I have to do, Jenny," Clint said, suddenly sure that she knew the outlaw's whereabouts. "Where is he?"

She hesitated a moment, then said, "He's in my room, upstairs from the saloon."

SIXTEEN

Jenny nervously took Clint around to the back of the saloon and showed him the rear entrance.

"There's a stairway inside," she said. "You go up, and my room is the first door on the left."

"Is there a number on it?"

"No."

"First on the left."

"Right."

"He's there alone?"

"Who would he be with?" she asked. "I'm with you."

"I thought maybe one of the other girls . . ."

"Not in my room."

"Where does he think you are?"

"Working," she said. "I told him I'd come up as soon as I finished."

"Did you tell him when that would be?"

"About an hour."

"So when I open the door he's going to think it's you," Clint said, half to himself.

"He still might go for his gun," she said.

71

Clint frowned. She was still trying to get him to kill Rufus King.

"I'll be ready," he said.

"What should I do?"

"Go back to work," Clint said.

"How will I know when you got him?"

"I'll let you know."

"What will you do with him if you don't kill him?" she asked.

He thought for a moment, then said, "I'll take him over to the sheriff's office."

"There is no sheriff!" she exclaimed, as if he were stupid.

"But there are still jail cells," he said. "I'll put him in one of them."

Her eyes brightened. "That's a good idea."

"Thanks."

He started to go in, but she grabbed his arm and said, "Wait!"

"What is it?"

"He's gonna think I told you where he was."

"You did."

"But what if he—"

"Look, don't worry," Clint said. "I won't say anything about you. I'll just tell him I was checking all the rooms."

"But will he believe you?"

"Once I get him, Jenny, he's going to Judge Parker's court," Clint said. "You know what will happen after that, right?"

"Yes," she said, with satisfaction. "He'll hang."

"Most likely," Clint said. "Now go back to work; there's a good girl. I'll let you know when it's all over."

He turned to enter, and she was right behind him.

"No," he said, "you go in the *front* door."

"Oh, right. Good luck."

Impulsively, she gave him a kiss on the cheek for luck. He breathed in her fragrance and wished this was another time or place. When she'd come to his room he had briefly entertained the thought that maybe she was there for . . . well, another reason.

Maybe later, he thought, as he went in the back door. . . .

He went up the staircase quietly and didn't draw his gun until he was outside her room, first door on the left. He hesitated briefly, again remembering Stacy in Muskogee. What if Rufus had sent Jenny to him, and while he was kicking in the first door on the left, the killer was going to come out of the first door on the right and kill him?

Ah, he couldn't let one duplicitous saloon girl make him paranoid.

He turned the knob slowly, then swung the door open and stepped in.

SEVENTEEN

"Who the hell are you?" the scraggly looking youth sitting on the bed demanded.

"Are you Rufus King?"

"What if I am? You got the wrong room, friend."

"Keep your hands where I can see them, Rufus."

The young killer was wearing his gun, even while sitting on the bed waiting for a woman.

"What's this all about?"

Clint kept him covered with his right hand while taking out the badge with the left and showing it to him.

"Aw, shit," Rufus King said, "you gotta be kiddin' me. She turned me in?"

"Who?"

"You know who. Jenny."

Clint shook his head and put the badge away.

"I don't know any— Wait a minute. You mean the girl downstairs?"

"Who else would I mean?" he asked. "Didn't she tell you where I was?"

"I haven't spoken to her since this afternoon," Clint

75

said. "I was checking all of these rooms, and I guess I got lucky."

"Maybe not so lucky," Rufus said.

"You want to try for your gun, Rufus? Or take it out and drop it on the floor? Your choice."

Rufus seemed to consider the proposition, then grinned, shrugged, and said, "Not while you got me covered. Now, if you wanted to holster that thing . . ."

"You'd end up dead," Clint finished for him, "and then I couldn't find out what I need to know."

"Which is?"

"Get rid of the gun first—left-handed."

Rufus reached across his body, removed his gun from his holster, and tossed it on the floor.

"Satisfied?"

"For now," Clint said.

"So whataya wanna know?" Rufus asked. "Maybe we can make a deal."

"I'm not making any deals," Clint said. "I'm taking you to see Judge Parker."

"So he can string me up?"

"So he can see that justice is done," Clint corrected him. "But first you're going to tell me where Scott Borton is."

"Who?"

"Scott Borton," Clint said. "The kid you recruited from a ranch just outside of Muskogee."

"You wanna know where the rest of my gang is? Is that it?"

"That would help."

"Well, see, then we can deal. I'll tell you where they are, and you let me go."

"Uh-uh," Clint said. "The rest of the gang is no good without the ringleader. I show up with them and Parker will just send me right back out to look for you, and I'm not doing that again. I'm doing him this one favor."

"Favor? You work for Parker and you call it a favor?" Rufus asked.

"I don't work for him," Clint said.

"You got a badge."

"I just carry it to shut him up. This is a favor for him, and one for Scott Borton's father."

"There you go with that Borton again. How do you know I got him?"

"He's in your gang."

"Well, he could be. See, I don't know that everybody in my gang told me their right names. What's this Borton look like."

"Nineteen, like you. Blond."

"Blond, hmmm," Rufus said.

"All right," Clint said, "I'll give you some time to think about it."

"Okay, fine. Come back later, when I'm done with the girl."

"You're done now. Let's go."

"Where are you taking me?"

"To jail."

"Ha!" Rufus snorted. "The joke's on you. This town ain't got no lawman."

"But it's got a jail," Clint said, "and that's where I'm taking you."

"The jail's closed."

"Get on your feet," Clint said. "We'll open it."

EIGHTEEN

Clint took Rufus King out of the building the way he had come in, the young killer's gun tucked into his own gun belt. He walked him across the street to the jail without attracting attention.

"Stop," he said in front of the jailhouse.

"Now what?"

"Now we go in."

"It's locked."

"How do you know?"

"It's been locked for weeks, months."

"We'll unlock it."

"How?"

"Stand over there, in front of the boarded-up window."

Rufus did as he was told.

Clint moved to the door and, with his left hand, turned the doorknob. He wasn't surprised when the door opened.

"Not locked," he said.

"How did you know?"

"You lock the door when you're trying to protect something," Clint said. "There's nothing in here to protect." He pushed the door open. "Inside."

79

Rufus went in ahead of Clint, who had a match ready. He struck it and told Rufus, "Stand still. You're backlit by the moonlight so I couldn't miss."

He found a storm lamp and lit it, bathing the room in yellow light.

"Close the door."

Rufus did.

The place smelled musty and was full of dust. The desk was in a corner, and on the wall behind it hung the key to the cells.

"Let's go and find you a nice cell," he said.

He took the key from the peg on the wall and marched Rufus into the cell block. There were two, and the doors were wide open.

"What if the locks don't work?" Rufus asked.

"We'll figure something out. Get in."

"Which one?"

"You pick," Clint said, "since you'll probably be here for a while."

"I don't think so," Rufus said, stepping into the near cell. "Once my boys hear I'm in here they'll come and get me."

"Good," Clint said, closing the cell door. "Then I won't have to go looking for them, will I?"

He turned the key in the lock and then tried the door. It held.

"Well, well," Clint said, "nice and secure."

"You think so?" Rufus asked. "The walls probably just need one good kick."

He turned and kicked the wall, then kicked it again. It held fast.

"Maybe not," he said, grinning.

"Have a seat, Rufus," Clint said. "You're going to be here awhile."

As Clint turned to leave Rufus dropped onto a pallet and raised some dust. He coughed and fanned it away, and now he wasn't grinning at all.

• • •

When Clint entered the saloon, Jenny came running over to him.

"Did you get him?"

"I got him."

She clapped her hands.

"Wonderful. Is he in jail?"

"Yes."

She turned and ran to the bartender.

"Rufus King is in jail."

"What?"

"He's in the jail!"

"Jenny—" Clint said, but it was too late.

"This man's a deputy, and he arrested him and put him in our jail."

Jake, the bartender, looked at Clint.

"Is that true?" he asked.

"Yes, but don't—"

"Hey, everybody!" Jake shouted. "Rufus King is in our jail! This feller just put him there."

And then everyone was shouting and yelling and asking questions. In the middle of melee, Clint quietly backed out the doors and went back to the jail.

There'd be no sleeping in a comfortable hotel bed tonight. Then he smiled, because the hotel bed hadn't been comfortable at all.

NINETEEN

Clint dusted off the chair and the desk in the sheriff's office, hung his hat on a peg, kept his gun belt on. He didn't bother taking down the boards that had been nailed across the window. Word would get around soon enough without a light in the window announcing it to the town.

"Hey, is that you, deputy?" Rufus shouted from the cell block.

Clint walked into the back.

"It's me, but don't call me deputy."

"Oh, that's right," Rufus sneered. "You ain't a deputy, you're just carryin' that badge as a favor to the Hangin' Judge."

"What do you want, King?"

"I'm hungry."

"It's late," Clint said, "everything's closed. I'll get you some breakfast in the morning."

"How long do you think you can keep me here?"

"Until I take you back to Fort Smith."

"And when is that gonna be?"

"As soon as I find out what's happened to Scott Borton and where he is."

Rufus put his hands behind his head and leaned back on the pallet.

"Well, then I guess it ain't exactly in my best interests to tell you, is it?"

"Anything you do to cooperate—"

"Is gonna keep me from gettin' hung?"

"Probably not."

"You know," Rufus said, "the judge really has no cause to hang me."

"Would you like to explain that?"

"It's simple," Rufus said. "I ain't never killed any-body."

"That's not the way I hear it."

"It's true," Rufus said. "I let the other fellas do all the killin'."

"What about the raping?"

"Well," Rufus said, "a fella's got to have some fun."

"That's what you call raping other men's wives? Fun?" Clint asked.

"Don't forget daughters," Rufus said. "We rape men's daughters, too."

"I'm not going to listen to this," Clint said, and started to walk out.

"In fact, we got this new kid with us, Cherry Boy, we call him," Rufus said. "He took to the rapin' and the killin' real quick. He *really* likes it."

"And what's this Cherry Boy look like?" Clint asked. "Does he have blond hair?"

"Well, now, that's hard to say," Rufus said, frowning in mock concentration. "Ya see, Cherry Boy keeps his hat on most of the time. I can't rightly say what color his hair is."

"You expect me to believe that you just let the others do the killing?"

"I don't like killin', mister— Hey, you never did tell me your name."

Clint hesitated, then thought, *Why not?*

"It's Adams," he said. "Clint Adams."

"Clint . . . whoa," Rufus said, leaping off his pallet and coming to the bars. He hung on to them and asked, "You mean I went and got myself arrested by the one and only Gunsmith?"

"What's the difference who arrested you?"

"This is gonna make me famous!" he exclaimed gleefully. "Yes, sir, they're gonna wanna write my story. Writer fellas from New York will come and talk to me in my cell before I hang."

"You're dreaming, Rufus."

"Hey," Rufus said, "I'm just a nineteen-year-old kid, and us kids gotta have dreams, don't we?"

"Get some sleep, Rufus," Clint said, "and I hope you have nightmares."

TWENTY

Clint slept in the sheriff's chair with his feet up on the sheriff's desk. A couple of times he started awake as he almost fell, but then he repositioned himself and dozed again.

Rufus King either slept through the night or simply kept quiet. Maybe he was trying to think of a way out. One time Clint awoke and thought that maybe he *had* gotten out, so he went and checked. In that instance Rufus was there, asleep.

When he woke in the morning, Clint was hungry. It was too early, however, for a café to be open, so he busied himself looking through the old desk. He found some letters sent from the East, written in a feminine hand and addressed to Peter Sykes. He didn't read them. Apparently, Sheriff Sykes was originally from the East; one would assume that he had gone back there.

He found some posters and began to go through them. Some of the faces on them he knew were already in prison or dead. He didn't come across one for Rufus King. Maybe one hadn't been printed, yet, or Sheriff Sykes had left before it had.

Finally, hunger got the better of him and he left the office to find an open café. He found one a block away, led there by the smells emanating from it. He asked the waiter for two plates of steak and eggs that he could take with him to the jail.

"The jail?" the man asked. "The jail is closed up."

"Not anymore, I'm afraid," Clint said.

"You have a prisoner at the jail?"

"That's right."

The man frowned.

"Are you the new sheriff?"

"No," Clint said. He hadn't wanted to, but he took the badge Judge Parker had given him out of his pocket and showed it to the man. "I'm just passing through, and I'm using it."

"All right, Marshal," the waiter said. "Two plates comin' up."

The man went into the kitchen, and Clint heard raised voices a few moments later.

"I don't know," he heard the man say.

"Well, *ask* him!" a woman's voice insisted.

The waiter appeared a moment later, smiling nervously. He was a small man, about five six, probably didn't weigh a hundred and forty pounds, seemed to be in his mid-forties. Clint wondered what the wife looked like. She *sounded* bigger than him.

"It's comin' up, Marshal," he said, "but, uh, my wife—she's the cook—wanted me to ask, uh, if we'd be getting paid for these meals?"

"Well, of course I intend to pay for them," Clint said. "Why wouldn't I?"

"Well, it's just that, this close to the jail—well, the last sheriff used to eat here for, uh, free, and—"

"Tell your wife I'll pay full price for the meals," Clint said, "and I would also appreciate a large pot of coffee."

"Large pot," the man said, happily, "comin' up."

"And make it strong."

The man clapped his hands together and said, "That's just the way my missus makes it, strong."

"Good."

Clint waited about fifteen minutes and then the waiter appeared with a covered tray. He removed the cloth from over the two meals and showed Clint not only steak and eggs, but potatoes and biscuits as well. Next to that on the tray was a large, black pot of coffee, and two thick mugs.

"Will this do, Marshal?"

"That'll do fine, Mr., uh—"

"Everett, Marshal," the man said, "Carl Everett."

"Thank you, Mr. Everett, and please thank your wife for me," Clint said. They exchanged money for the tray. "Tell her for me she outdid herself."

"I'll tell her, Marshal," Everett said. "I surely will."

Clint nodded and left with the tray.

As he entered the office moments later, he heard Rufus King shouting from the cell block.

"Damn it, can't you hear me? Am I gonna starve back here?"

Clint stopped at the desk, removed one plate from the tray, and left it on the desk. Then he poured one of the mugs full, and left the other mug and the pot on the desk, along with one set of silverware. That done, he carried the tray into the back.

"Rise and shine, Rufus," he called out. "Breakfast."

"Its about time," Rufus King said, his arms hanging out of the cell as he leaned on the bars.

"Step back if you want this food, Rufus," Clint warned. "Try anything and I'll put a bullet in your leg."

"I ain't gonna try anything, Adams," Rufus said, "least-ways, not until after I eat. Damn! That smells good."

He backed away and Clint unlocked the door, set the tray on the floor and pushed it into the cell, then closed and locked the door.

"You've got a knife and a fork there, Rufus," Clint said.

"Don't get any ideas about using them on anything but that steak."

"Steak?" Rufus asked. He pounced on the tray. "By golly, you did, you brought me steak and eggs? Hell, man, if I knew they fed you this good in jail I'da got myself arrested a long time ago."

"Just shut up and eat it, Rufus," Clint said. "And keep quiet about it while I eat mine."

Rufus sipped the coffee and his eyes went wide.

"By golly," he said, again, "I sure am tired of trail coffee."

Clint usually made his trail coffee himself, so he kind of liked it. When he got to his desk, though, and sipped Mrs. Everett's, he had to admit it was good. He only hoped the rest of the meal was as good.

TWENTY-ONE

"So how long we gonna wait?" Cherry Boy demanded.

"It's only been two nights," Louis Davis said.

"And half a day," Cherry Boy said. He looked at Sam Sampson. "How long does he usually take?"

Sampson chewed the inside of his cheek.

"Lucky?" Cherry Boy said. "You know how long he usually takes?"

Lucky Davis shrugged, so Cherry Boy turned back to Sampson, who'd known Rufus King the longest.

In point of fact, Sam Sampson was the only one who knew that Rufus had never even been with the gal in Carlyle, Jenny Morse. He usually rode in, sniffed around her all night, and then came back the next day acting like he got laid.

"Might be he shoulda been back by now," Sampson finally said.

"Then maybe we better go in after him, huh?" Cherry Boy suggested. "He might be in trouble."

"How much trouble could he get inta?" Lucky asked. "Ain't no law in Carlyle. Rufus himself run the last sheriff out."

"How do we know they didn't get a new one by now?" Cherry Boy asked. "Come on, Sam. We got to go in and check on him."

Sampson chewed his cheek a little more.

"Rufus told us to wait here, Sam," Louis said. "He's gonna be awful mad we don't listen."

"He's gonna be awful made if he's in trouble and we don't help him," Cherry Boy pointed out.

"I'll go," Sampson finally said. "The three of you stay here."

They were using a box canyon as a hideout: one way in and one way out.

"While I'm gone, stand watch on the mouth of the canyon, taking turns," Sampson said. "I shouldn't be gone long. Just long enough to see what's goin' on."

"Don't let him see you checkin' on him, Sam," Lucky warned him. "He'll be madder than a whole nest of hornets if he sees ya."

"Don't worry," Sampson said. "If he ain't in any trouble, he ain't gonna see me."

"I think we should all go," Cherry Boy said.

The two Davis boys looked at their newest gang member and shook their heads.

"If there's trouble," Sampson said, "I'll know soon enough, and I'll come back and get all of ya. For now just stay put."

"We'll stay," Lucky said, "Don't worry."

Cherry Boy shook his head and walked away as Sampson headed for his horse. In the short time since he'd joined this gang, he realized he had already surpassed them. They were holding him back, but he decided to wait a little while longer. If Rufus King had been captured, or was dead, it wouldn't take too much effort to make this gang his own.

Just a little longer. . . .

TWENTY-TWO

Later that day, Clint brought the tray and coffeepot back to the café and told Carl Everett—quite honestly—that the meals had been fine.

"That's good, Marshal," Everett said, "real good. You want to stay for some lunch?"

"No," Clint said, "I've got to get back to the jail. Nobody's watching the prisoner."

"Uh, Marshal?"

"Yes?"

"We, uh, heard some talk in here that the prisoner you got is, uh, Rufus King. Is that true?"

"It's true, Mr. Everett."

Everett's eyes widened.

"What are you gonna do with him?"

"I'm going to take him to Fort Smith to stand before Judge Parker."

"Are you leavin' soon?"

"Don't know, Mr. Everett," Clint said. "I haven't decided yet."

"Well, until you do," Everett said, "you come on back here and we'll feed y'all."

"I appreciate it, Mr. Everett."

"You can call me Carl, Marshal."

"All right, Carl. My name is Clint Adams."

"Clint . . . Adams?"

He left Carl Everett standing there with his mouth open, wondering why he'd gone ahead and introduced himself like that. It'd be all over town soon, who he was and who he had in the cell.

He turned and headed back to the jail.

He seated himself behind the desk and leaned back to do some thinking. If he simply took Rufus King back to Fort Smith, Judge Parker would probably be happy to hang the young man, but that wouldn't do Dave Borton any good. He needed to get King to tell him about Scott Borton or tell him where the other members of the gang were. Either that or sit tight and see if the others came to get Rufus out. They'd know about his capture soon enough. It remained to be seen if they could do anything about it without him leading them.

Of course, that could take days, and he couldn't afford to leave the jail unattended anymore, not even for the short walk down the street to the café. Once word got around about who he had there, and who he was, he might have more to worry about than Rufus King's gang members. Once again he had to be careful he didn't run afoul of someone who just wanted to try him, or someone who wanted to prove to Rufus King they should be part of his gang.

What he needed was a deputy, even if it was just for a couple of days. Somebody to watch the jail while he went for food, or somebody he could send for food.

Question was, where was he going to find a deputy in the town the size of Carlyle, once word got out? And how was he going to find one when he couldn't even leave the jail?

By locking Rufus King up he'd succeeded in making

himself a prisoner, as well, as long as they stayed in Carlyle.

It was getting on toward early evening when there was a knock on the door. Clint got up from the desk, drew his gun, and went to the door.

"Who is it?"

"Carl Everett, Marshal."

"What can I do for you, Carl?"

There was a moment's hesitation, and then the man said, "I brought you some supper."

Clint unlocked the door, cracked it open, and peered out. Carl was standing there holding a cloth-covered tray with a pot of coffee on it. There was also a large mug of beer.

"I figured you'd be hungry by now," he said.

"You figured right, Carl," Clint replied. He opened the door wider. "Come on in."

Carl Everett entered, and after a quick look outside, Clint closed the door and turned to face the man.

"You can put it down on the desk, Carl," Clint said. "What do I owe you?"

Carl told him and he paid him.

"I'd give it to you for free, Marshal, seein' as how you're the law and all, but my wife . . ."

"I understand, Carl. I thank you for bringing it over."

"Thought you could probably use a beer as well as some coffee. Best you drink it while's it's still some cold."

Clint picked up the beer and took a few grateful swallows.

"Didn't bring one for the prisoner. Didn't think you'd want him drinkin'."

"You're right about that."

Carl stood there awkwardly for a few moments, and Clint wondered what was on his mind.

"Can I do somethin' else for you, Carl? I'm afraid I won't be able to bring the tray back to you. I can't risk leaving the jail unattended."

"T-that's what I wanted to talk to you about, Marshal," Carl stammered.

"What's that, Carl?"

"Well, you need someone to help you. I wanna be, you know, your deputy."

"I don't have the authority to make you a deputy, Carl," Clint said. "Can you use a gun?"

"I can use a shotgun," Carl said. "You need someone to spell you. I can do that."

Clint hesitated. He *did* need someone to spell him, and all they had to do was sit in the office for a little while each day.

"I don't have any guns in here, Carl," he said, looking around.

"I have a shotgun, Marshal," the little man said. "I can use my own."

"What's your wife say about this?"

"Well . . . she's not happy, but I told her it's somethin' I got to do."

Clint hated to turn Everett down, especially since he seemed to be standing up to his wife in order to do this.

"All right, Carl."

"You mean it?"

"I mean it," Clint said. "Come back later to get the tray, and bring your shotgun. I'll let you spell me for an hour or two."

"Thanks, Marshal," Everett said. "You sure won't regret this."

"I'm sure I won't, Carl," Clint said, but he was thinking he *hoped* he wouldn't.

TWENTY-THREE

When Clint gave Rufus his meal, he told him that there'd be another man coming in to look after him.

"You managed to find yourself a deputy?" the young outlaw asked. "In this town?"

"He's not going to be deputized," Clint said. "He's just somebody who's going to help—and he'll have a shotgun, so don't try anything."

"What can I try from in here?" Rufus asked, innocently. "Besides, I just have to wait here until my boys come and get me. You'll need more than some storekeeper with a shotgun when they get here."

"Eat your dinner," Clint said, and went back into the office to eat his own.

Rufus King seemed fairly sure that his gang would come to town to free him. Clint should have been pleased with that. If they came to town, he'd be able to identify Scott Borton. Of course, Scott would be one of at least four outlaws he would have to deal with. Even if he could talk Scott into going home, he'd still have three more of them to handle.

He'd gone up against three- and four-to-one odds before, but that didn't mean he had to like it.

When Sam Sampson rode into Carlyle, it was getting dark. He didn't want anyone to know who he was or why he was there, so he was going to have to try to find out what he wanted by listening and by keeping his eyes open. The best place to do that was in the saloon.

He knew which saloon Jenny Morse worked in, so he tied his horse up in front of it and went inside. He went to the bar and ordered a beer, then used the mirror behind the bar to look around. It didn't take long for him to spot Jenny. She was easily the best-looking girl working the floor.

He needed to turn around to see the rest of the saloon, and he didn't see Rufus King anywhere. He knew that Rufus had never before made it to Jenny's room, but maybe this was finally the time. Maybe he was up there waiting for her to get off work.

Who was he kidding? Both he and Rufus knew that the girl didn't want anything to do with Rufus, or anyone like him. Rufus always got mad when Sampson pointed this out, but he wasn't stupid.

Nevertheless, Sampson nursed his beer, watched Jenny, and kept his ears open, and before long he heard all he needed to hear.

When Carl Everett returned later in the evening he had his shotgun in tow. Clint let him in and examined the weapon, a greener that had seen better days but was functional.

Before he left, Clint gave Everett his instructions.

"I'll only be gone as long as it takes to get a bath and collect some things from my hotel room."

"Right."

"There's no reason for you to go back there and talk to him."

"Okay."

"Not even if he calls you. Understand?"

"I understand."

"If you go back there, he'll try to trick you, or imtimidate you."

"He won't," Everett said firmly.

"That's right, he won't, because you're not going back there, right?"

"Right."

"When I come back I'll knock and identify myself."

"How will you knock?" Everett asked.

"I'll just knock, Carl," Clint said. "You'll say, 'Who is it?' and I'll identify myself."

"How will I know it's you?"

"You'll recognize my voice."

"What if I don't?"

"Then don't open the door."

"Right."

When Clint left the jail he wasn't at all sure it was a good idea to leave Carl Everett there, but he needed a bath, and he wanted to collect his saddlebags and his rifle. He also wanted to stop by the hotel for a beer and to talk briefly with Jenny.

When he entered the saloon he wasn't at all ready for the reception he got.

"Hey, there he is!" the bartender yelled. "The man who put Rufus King behind bars!"

There was cheering and backslapping and people offering to buy him drinks. In all the confusion Sam Sampson leaned over and asked the bartender, "Who is that feller?"

"That's the marshal who put Rufus King in jail."

"I thought the jail was closed."

"He opened it."

The bartender turned away; Sampson grabbed his sleeve. "But who is he?" he asked. "What's his name?"

"Adams," the bartender said, "Clint Adams."

Sampson whistled silently, and before the commotion died down he sneaked out to his horse and rode out of town as hard and as fast as he could.

TWENTY-FOUR

Clint had to get out of the saloon. The crush of bodies to get to him to touch him or buy him a drink was too cloying. He signaled to Jenny that he wanted to talk to her and she nodded. He then made his way to the door and got out of there before anyone realized he was gone.

For a nineteen year old, Rufus King sure aroused a lot of reaction from the people of Carlyle.

He went to his hotel room and wondered if he should give it up; then he decided to keep it and just take his saddlebags and rifle to the jail. He was almost ready to leave when there was a knock on the door.

It was Jenny, and her eyes were shining.

"Wha—" he said, but she was all over him, her mouth avidly seeking his, her hands down between his legs.

"Jenny—"

"Were you ever so excited you just couldn't stand it?" she asked him, with her mouth still pressed to his. "You just had to have it?"

He had been, on occasion, and her hands on him and her mouth on his neck was getting him there now.

"Jenny . . ."

"Shhh," she said, still with her sweet-tasting mouth pressed to his. "Later, later." She pulled his shirt open and kissed his chest. "Later," she repeated, and then slid to her knees and undid his trousers.

In no time his pants and underwear were down around his ankles and she had his erect penis in her hands, cooing to it, rubbing it against her pale cheek, and then, finally, taking him into her hot mouth.

He'd had to remove his gun belt quickly and was holding it in his hand, unwilling to put it down in light of recent events. Her head moved quickly as she sucked him, taking him deeply into her mouth and then sliding him along her lips until he was almost out, and then taking him deep again.

Abruptly, she put her hands against his thighs and pushed him back so that he landed on the bed. She pulled off his boots, then the rest of his clothes, and when he was naked she wrenched off her own clothes and mounted him.

Her skin was pale and hot, her breasts full and rounded and pink tipped. They swayed in front of his face as she rode him up and down. He'd thought her mouth was hot, but the depths of her were steaming. She was so excited and wet that she left a sweet trail on his thighs as she bounced up and down on him, her mouth open, her head thrown back. He cupped her buttocks, leaving the gun belt on the bed next to him, then slid his hands to her hips, then up her rib cage to her breasts. He held them to his mouth so he could suck her nipples, bite the tender flesh around them, leaving little nip marks on her, and then when she gasped and he could feel the pleasure surging through her, he lifted his buttocks from the bed and relaxed his own will so that he exploded inside of her. . . .

"That was wild," she said, lying next to him. "I don't think I've ever been that excited before."

"I wish it was me," he said, rubbing one hand up and down her thigh.

"Oh, but it was," she said, rolling into him so that the length of her was pressed to him. "You're the one who put Rufus away and made me safe, you're the one who was at the center of that . . . that melee in the saloon. You're the one who's brought excitement to the whole town."

"Just for putting some nineteen-year-old kid in jail?" he asked.

"Ever since Rufus and his gang started raising hell, he's been using this town as his rest stop," she said. "Everyone was afraid of him because he said his gang was just outside of town. He ate, drank, and took whatever he wanted without ever paying a cent, and now that's over."

He slid his hand over her taut butt and said, "I wish that was true."

"What do you mean?"

"Well, his gang is still out there," Clint said, "and once they hear he's in jail they'll come to get him out."

She rolled away from him and sat up. She hugged herself, folding her arms across her breasts.

"You said you wouldn't let him get away."

"And I won't," Clint said, "but I could use a little help."

"You're not going to get any help from this town, Clint," she said. "The men here are too afraid."

"I already have help," he said. "That's why I'm here right now and not at the jail . . . but I do have to get back there."

He got off the bed and started collecting his clothes.

"Who's helping?"

"A fellow named Everett, Carl Everett."

"Him and his wife run the café."

"That's right."

"How can he help?"

"Well, right now he's sitting over in the jail with a shotgun while I'm here with you," Clint said, getting dressed, "and I'm supposed to be coming right back after a bath."

"A bath?"

"Well, I can forget that, now," he said.

"Wasn't I better than a bath?" she asked.

"Jenny," he said, "you were a lot better than a bath."

She smiled and dropped her arms away from her luscious breasts.

"Come back to bed," she said. "He can wait a little longer."

"I'd like to," he said, "but I can't. You want me to make sure Rufus doesn't get out, don't you?"

That put a damper on her ardor, and she crossed her arms in front of her again.

"I don't ever want him to get out," she said. "Couldn't you just, like, shoot him while he tried to escape?"

"I don't work that way."

"No, I guess not."

She got off the bed and started to get dressed.

"Well," she said, "I'm afraid Mr. Everett is probably the only man in town who'll be willing to help you, and I know why."

"Why?"

"It's the only way he can get away from that wife of his."

Clint left his torso bare and used the water from the pitcher on the dresser to fill a basin and clean himself off.

"What does she look like?"

Once again wearing her dress, her hair disheveled, Jenny sat on the bed with her hands clasped in her lap.

"Nobody knows," she said. "Nobody's seen her in years. I don't think she ever leaves that kitchen."

He dried off and donned a fresh shirt from his saddlebag.

"Well, whatever his reasons I'm glad to have him," Clint said. "Maybe he'll shame some of the other men in this town into volunteering."

She laughed and said, "You don't know the men in this town if you think that."

"Come on," he said, "I have to go."

They left the room together and walked down to the lobby.

"I'll wait here and leave after you," she said. "Maybe before you leave town with Rufus we can . . . get together again?"

"I'd like that a lot, Jenny."

"Uh, when will you be leaving town with him?"

"I can't say for a fact," Clint said. "Catching him was just part of the job, for me."

"But you won't let him out, right?"

"Right."

"I mean, you won't let him get away?"

"Not a chance."

"Because if he does, he'll kill me."

He touched her cheek and said, "I'd never let that happen, Jenny."

She touched his hand, then took a deep breath and nodded. He smiled at her and headed back to the jail, refreshed in an entirely different way than he'd intended.

TWENTY-FIVE

Clint knocked on the door to the sheriff's office. There was no answer. He knocked again. He wondered if Rufus King had been able to lure Carl Everett back to his cell, and if he'd managed to get himself out and put Everett in his place—or worse. What was he thinking, leaving a man who was dominated by his wife in charge of a prisoner? If King were gone and Everett locked up, or worse, he had no one to blame but himself.

He knocked a third time.

He thought he heard some movement from within. Was King waiting for him, armed with Everett's shotgun?

"W-who is it?" Everett's voice was timid, as if he expected the person knocking to be his wife.

"It's me, Carl, Clint Adams."

There was a moment's hesitation. "W-who?"

He'd introduced himself, hadn't he? Hadn't he told Everett his name? Or did the man simply think of him as the deputy marshal?

"Carl, it's Clint Adams. I told you not to let anyone but me in."

"H-how do I know it's you?"

107

"I told you that you'd recognize my voice, remember?"

Clint waited, then heard the bolt slide back; the door opened a crack. He saw Carl Everett's eye, and then the door opened wider and Everett's relieved face came into view.

"Oh, it's you."

"Carl," Clint said, "if you didn't recognize my voice why'd you open the door?"

"Well," Everett replied, "you said it was you."

"Yes, I did," Clint said, slipping inside. He turned, closed the door, and locked it.

"How did it go?" he asked Everett.

"Fine," the man said. "I did what you said. I didn't go back there, even when he called me."

"He called you?"

"Well, he called out," Everett said. "Not to *me*, but h-he called out. I didn't go back. Do you think maybe he hurt himself and needed help? Did I do the right thing?"

"You did exactly the right thing, Carl," Clint said, patting the man on the back. "You can head back home now. Your wife is probably worried."

"My wife . . ." Everett said, as if Clint had reminded him that he had one. "Ah, I could stay longer, if you like. Do you have any other errands to run?"

"No," Clint said, putting his saddlebags and rifle down on the desk, "I don't."

"Shall I bring breakfast by in the morning?"

"That sounds like a good idea."

"What would you like?"

"Whatever your wife makes will be fine, Carl."

"Well . . . all right . . . I guess I'll go home, then."

"That sounds like a good idea."

"Yeah," Everett said, as if to say, *Maybe it sounds like a good idea to* you.

He turned and headed for the door.

"Carl?"

"Yes?" The man turned, looking hopefully at Clint, hoping he was going to ask him to stay.

"Don't you want to take your shotgun?"

The other man's face fell.

"Oh," he said. "Well, no, I might as well leave it here. I'll be needing it. I wouldn't, uh, want to take it home."

Clint wondered if Everett was afraid he'd use the shotgun on his wife if he took it home with him.

"Okay," he said. "Suit yourself."

Everett headed for the door, the stopped and turned.

"Do you play checkers, Clint?"

"What? Sure, I play checkers."

"I'll bring a board by tomorrow when I come. Maybe we can play."

"Sure, Carl," Clint said, "I'd like to play."

That seemed to cheer the other man up some as he opened the door and headed for home, which, Clint thought, was apparently the last place he wanted to go.

TWENTY-SIX

It was dark when Sam Sampson got back to the hideout where the other gang members were waiting. During his absence, Cherry Boy had been doing a lot of talking to one Davis brother or the other, whichever one wasn't on watch at the time.

"What kind of a leader leaves his men to go and chase a woman?" he asked Lucky.

"Rufus is the leader," was all Lucky would say, with a shrug.

"Well, if I was the leader I sure wouldn't be leavin' my men to sit around and do nothin' when there's things to be done," he told Louis.

"What would you be doin'?" Louis asked.

"I'd be out findin' things for us to do," Cherry Boy said. "Things that would be fun, but also profitable for us. Seems to me we should have more money in our pockets. I don't think any of us would object to that, do you?"

"Not me," Louis said.

"Not me," Lucky said, separately.

So by the time Sam Sampson got back, Cherry Boy had

pretty much gotten the Davis boys around to his way of thinking.

Lucky was on watch when Sampson got back.

"You better come down to the cabin," he told Lucky. "We got trouble."

"What kind of trouble?" Lucky asked.

"The kind that's got Rufus locked up in jail."

"Wha—"

Before he could ask any more question, Sampson rode off toward the cabin. Lucky climbed down from the rock he'd been keeping watch from and hurriedly followed on foot.

After Everett left the office, Rufus King called out to Clint.

"What do you want, Rufus?" Clint called back.

"Some water would be nice."

"Yeah, it would," Clint said, almost to himself. Also, he thought, a coffeepot.

"Don't have any," he called back.

"Some coffee?"

"Nope."

"What kind of jail is this?"

Clint walked to the door so he could look at Rufus in his cell.

"The kind that was closed up until yesterday," Clint said. "I'll have to get some water and a coffeepot tomorrow."

"Not that I figure on bein' here long," King said.

"I'm sure you don't."

"And who was that yahoo that was here before?" the outlaw asked. "Wouldn't even talk to me."

"That's because he's not supposed to talk to you," Clint said.

"What kind of deputy is that, won't even talk to a fella?"

"He's just somebody who wants to help, Rufus," Clint

said. "Wants to make sure you reach Judge Parker's court safely."

"That was what you wanted, you woulda took me there by now," King said, hanging on the bars. "What are you really after, Adams?"

"I want to make sure you don't corrupt any more nineteen year olds, Rufus."

Rufus King cackled, almost like an old man.

"Corrupt? Me? I ain't corruptin' nobody who don't want to be corrupted."

"Scott Borton didn't ask to be corrupted."

"Yer real concerned for yer friend's boy, ain't you?" King asked.

"That's right."

"That's what yer really after."

Clint didn't reply.

"I tell you what," Rufus King said, his tone dropping low, as if he were afraid someone would overhear them. "You let me loose, and I'll tell you where to find the boy."

"So he is part of your gang," Clint said. "Is he this 'Cherry Boy' you were talking about?"

"I ain't sayin' he is, and I ain't sayin' he ain't. I'm just tryin' to make a bargain with you, here."

"I'm not making any deals, Rufus."

"See?" Rufus said. "I'm tryin' to help you but I ain't gettin' no cooperation."

"Why don't you just tell me where your gang is holed up," Clint said.

"Oh, I won't have to tell you," Rufus assured him. "They'll be here soon enough. Them boys is gonna miss me, 'cause they need somebody to tell them when it's time to wipe their asses. They're dumb as stumps, all of 'em."

"Dumb as stumps" did not describe the Scott Borton Clint had known.

"Yessir," he continued, "they gonna be comin' in here lookin' for me any time now, and you gonna need a whole lot more than some fella lookin' to be helpful.''

"If I need any help, Rufus," Clint said, "you're the one who's going to give me all I need.''

He left Rufus to ponder that one.

TWENTY-SEVEN

"How did that happen?" Louis Davis asked Sam Sampson.

"From what I could hear in the saloon, he got taken by Clint Adams."

"The Gunsmith?" Cherry Boy asked. His eyes glittered with excitement.

"Right."

"Jesus," Lucky said.

"From what I heard it sounds like Adams was sent by Judge Parker to get Rufus."

"Parker'll hang him!" Louis said.

"In a minute," Sampson said.

"So whatta we do?" Louis asked.

"We get him out," Lucky said. "Ain't that what you're thinkin', Sam?"

"That's what I'm thinkin'," Sampson said, with a nod.

"Now wait a minute," Cherry Boy said.

They all turned to face him.

"Let's think this through," he continued. "If we go in there and try to get him out, we have to go up against the Gunsmith."

"Right," Sampson said.

"I'm not as good with a gun as the Gunsmith," Cherry Boy said. "Are any of you?"

The other three exchanged a glance and then shook their heads.

"No," Sampson said, answering for all three.

"And I don't want to get killed for Rufus," Cherry Boy said. "Do you?"

"He's one of us," Lucky said.

"Is he?"

"He's the leader," Sampson said.

"The boys and I were talkin' while you were gone, Sam, about what kind of leader Rufus is."

Sampson looked at both Davis brothers accusingly.

"He did most of the talkin'," Louis said.

"We just listened . . . mostly."

"It don't matter," Cherry Boy said. "Sam, I ain't seen Rufus kill anybody since I've been with you. Have you ever seen him kill someone?"

Sampson frowned and then said, "Well, he must've . . ."

"Did you ever see him?"

"He *said* he did—"

"But did you ever *see* him do it?" Cherry Boy demanded. "Any of you?"

Again, the three exchanged a glance; again, Sampson said, "No."

"That's because he gets us to do it for him," Cherry Boy said. "I've seen each of you kill someone, and we all know I have. Does that really sound like Rufus is one of us?"

"Well . . ." Sampson said, and then looked at the others for help. Neither Lucky nor Louis Davis had anything to say.

"So what are you sayin' we should do?" Sampson asked.

"I say leave Rufus there and move on," Cherry Boy said. "We can get along real well without him."

"But . . . he'll be hanged."

"I say it's better he get hanged than I get killed tryin' to save him."

The other three remained silent.

"Any of you want to die to save Rufus?"

Again, no response.

"I didn't think so."

"But then . . ." Louis began.

"What, Louis?" Cherry Boy asked.

Louis looked at the other two and said. "But then we need a new leader."

"That's right," Cherry Boy agreed.

"Who's it gonna be?" Lucky asked.

"I elect Sam," Cherry Boy said.

"Me?" Sampson asked. "Why me?"

"Because you're smart enough to know this is the right thing to do."

"I don't want to be the leader," Sampson said forcefully.

"You don't?"

"Hell, no."

Cherry Boy looked at the Davis boys, the excitement of the moment growing inside of him.

"Lucky?"

"Me?" Lucky said. "Not me."

"Louis?"

"Sam and Lucky," Louis said, "they're both smarter than me. If they don't want to be the leader, I sure don't."

"Then we have two choices," Cherry Boy said.

"What?"

"We can either disband and go our separate ways," he said, "or I can become the leader."

"You?" Sam said. "You been with us the shortest time. Why should you be the leader?"

Cherry Boy turned to face Sampson head-on.

"Because I want it, Sam," Cherry Boy said, "and none of you does. And because I don't want to disband. I'm having too much fun with you boys."

The other three fell silent again.

"What do you say?" Cherry Boy asked. "*Do* we disband, or go on having fun . . . and get rich while we're doin' it?"

They were silent and then Louis said. "Well, I like the part about gettin' rich."

"Well . . . so do I," Lucky said.

Cherry Boy looked at Sam.

"What do you say, Sam?"

Sampson looked undecided, then he shook his head and said, "I guess you're the new leader, Cherry Boy."

The excitement inside of him had worked itself into a tight ball, and as Sam Sampson said those words the ball exploded and filled him with warmth and power.

"Then let's get started. . . ."

TWENTY-EIGHT

Clint knew he should have contacted Judge Parker by now to tell him that he had captured Rufus King. Of course, he had a perfect excuse not to have done so because Carlyle did not have a telegraph office. Judge Parker would have said that he should have simply taken the prisoner to the nearest town that did have a telegraph office, or he should have taken the prisoner right to Fort Smith.

Judge Parker would have been right, but neither one of those actions would have helped him find Scott Borton.

After several days, however, he was starting to wonder if he was doing the right thing by waiting for Rufus King's gang to come for him.

Rufus King, he noticed, was also getting impatient for his gang to come to town.

"Damn idiots," he said one morning, "probably can't even find their way here!"

On the morning of the fourth day, Carl Everett stepped into the sheriff's office, greeting Clint as he had the previous mornings. They had taken to playing checkers in the afternoons, which served to keep Everett away from home more often.

On this morning he asked Clint the same question he always did, dreading the answer.

"Leavin' today?"

"I don't know, Carl," Clint said, and this satisfied Everett. As long as Clint needed him, he could spend less time at home and tell his wife that he was doing his "civic duty."

"Adams!" Rufus King yelled. "Why don't you just take me to Fort Smith and get it over with. Be better than stayin' in this place."

"He might be right," Clint said.

"You don't think the gang is gonna come for him?" Everett asked.

"Doesn't look like it, Carl."

"So what are you gonna do?"

"I haven't decided yet," Clint said, "but right now I'm going to go take a bath."

"Another one?"

Clint frowned, then remembered that Everett thought he had taken a bath four days earlier, when what he had actually done was have sex with Jenny Morse. He hadn't seen Jenny since then, except at the saloon when he stopped in for a beer.

"Yeah," he said, "another one."

This time, though, he really did take a bath. There was a barbershop across from the hotel that had public bathtubs, and he went in there to soak in one of them.

The barber brought in some fresh hot water at one point and started talking, like barbers—and bartenders—do. Clint wasn't really listening. He was just soaking with a washcloth over his face as the barber poured more hot water into the tub, and then something the man said penetrated.

"Wait a minute," he said, taking the washcloth from his face. "What did you say?"

"I said I guess that Rufus King gang don't need Rufus as much as he thought," the big, jug-eared barber repeated.

"Why do you say that?"

"Well, they hit a homestead not six miles from here," the barber said. "Killed the husband, raped the wife and the sixteen-year-old daughter, then killed the wife."

"And what about the girl?"

"They took her with them."

"Where did you hear this?"

"Fella just tol' me while I cut his hair," the barber said.

"Where's this fella now?"

"Said he was goin' to the saloon."

Clint stood up abruptly, water running off his body as he stepped out of the tub.

"Hey," the man complained, "I just put more hot water in the tub."

"That's okay," Clint said, grabbing a towel. "I'm clean enough."

"You got to pay for it, though."

"I'll pay for it," Clint said, "don't worry."

But who was he going to pay back for the people the gang had killed while he was sitting on his butt in Carlyle? And how was he going to explain this to Judge Parker?

TWENTY-NINE

Clint marched over to the saloon, armed with a description of the man who had brought to town the news of the latest attack by the Rufus King gang. It was noon, and the saloon had not been open all that long. When he entered he found that he didn't really need the description. There was only one man standing at the bar.

"Mind if I ask you a few questions?" Clint asked, approaching the man.

He turned and looked at Clint.

"Long as I can finish my beer. Who are you?"

"My name's Clint Adams. I heard you brought some news to town about the Rufus King gang."

"Sure did," he said. "Up Jay City way they hit again. Killed a man and woman and took their sixteen-year-old daughter."

"Jay City?"

"Ain't much of a city, really," the man said. "Little town between here and Fort Smith."

"Any law there?"

"Sheriff and a deputy," the man said. "Ain't you the Gunsmith?"

"That's right."

"I heard you locked Rufus King up."

"That's what I did."

"Guess his gang don't need him to be doin' some damage."

"Looks that way."

"I come from Fort Smith," the man said. "Heard you were carrying a badge for Judge Parker."

"What else did you hear?"

"That's where I heard you locked King up."

If that was the case, then that meant that Judge Parker had heard the news, as well.

Clint looked the man up and down. He was fit, in his thirties, wore a gun that had seen some use.

"Mind if I ask your business?" Clint asked.

"I got a job waitin' for me in Kansas," the man said, "but I ain't in a hurry to get there. Why?"

"I could use some help."

"With Rufus King?"

Clint nodded.

"What kind of help?"

"I just need another man to watch the jail while I ride to Jay City."

"Gonna put the rest of the gang away?"

"I'm going to try."

The man swirled what was left at the bottom of his beer mug, studying it for a moment.

"What's the job pay?"

"Food and drink," Clint said. "It won't even be official, but when I get to Fort Smith I'll try to get some compensation for you out of Judge Parker."

"I heard he's pretty tight with money."

"I can pay you something out of my own pocket."

The man hesitated a moment, then said, "Naw, you don't have to do that."

"So you won't take the job?"

"Sure I will," the man said, "for the food and drink you

just mentioned.'' He put his mug down. ''I'll start with another beer.''

''I'll have one with you,'' Clint said, ''and then we can take a walk over to the jail.''

When Clint entered the jail with another man in tow, Carl Everett was surprised. He was also undecided about whether or not he should grab his shotgun.

''Relax, Carl,'' Clint said, ''this man's here to help. His name's Jackson, Roy Jackson.''

''Mr. Jackson.''

''Heard you been a big help, Mr. Everett,'' Jackson said. ''Also heard your wife is quite a cook.''

''She's a good one, all right.''

''Good,'' Jackson said. ''If food and drink is all I'm gonna get for this job, it better be good.''

''Job?''

''Roy's is going to split shifts with you, Carl.''

''Why?'' Everett asked. ''What are you gonna be doin', Clint?''

''I've got to ride to Jay City,'' Clint said. ''Seems Rufus's gang has struck without him.''

Everett looked surprised.

''Never heard that they did that before. They're usually quiet whenever Rufus is here.''

''Well, Rufus is locked up now,'' Clint said. ''That might be the difference. You fellas work out the schedule between you. I'm going to talk to Rufus.''

He left the two men to get acquainted and went back to Rufus King's cell.

''What's goin' on?'' King asked.

''Breaking in new help, Rufus,'' Clint said. ''I've got to go out and look for your gang.''

''About time,'' King said. ''Sons of bitches shoulda been here by now.''

''I don't think they're coming.''

''Why not?''

"I just heard they struck without you."

"*What?*"

That got King up off the cot and hanging on the bars, staring at Clint.

"What are you talkin' about? They can't do a thing without me."

"I guess they've decided that they can," Clint said. "They killed a man and a woman after raping the woman and a sixteen-year-old girl—and then they took the girl with them."

King made a face and said, "Cherry Boy."

"What about him?"

"He's been wantin' to take a girl with us when we leave, but I never wanted to do that."

"Why not?"

" 'Cause people forget about money or valuables, but when you take a person somebody always come lookin'."

"Like me."

Rufus King nodded.

"Tell me where they are, Rufus," Clint said. "Where's the hideout?"

King didn't answer.

"Come on, Rufus. They left you here to go to Fort Smith and hang. Don't you want revenge?"

The outlaw hesitated, then said, "I ain't gonna help you, Adams. I ain't gonna do it. You go and find them yourself."

"I'm going to do just that, Rufus," Clint said, "and then they're going to share the same gallows with you."

"That go for your friend's boy, too, Adams?" King taunted. "You gonna bring him back to hang, too?"

"If he's part of your gang," Clint said, "and if he killed that rancher and his wife and took their daughter, he'll pay just like the rest of you."

King didn't comment.

"Well?" Clint asked.

"Well what?"

"Is he part of your gang?"

Rufus King smirked and said, "Guess you're gonna have to find that out for yourself."

THIRTY

"You said you weren't gonna let him get out," Jenny said to Clint.

"I'm not."

"How are you gonna keep him in jail if you're not here?"

They were in his hotel room, in bed, and he was explaining why he had to leave the next day.

"I have two men watching him, Jenny."

"A storekeeper and a drifter," she scoffed. "What happens if his gang comes to town to get him? Them two ain't gonna stand against them the way you would."

"His gang isn't going to come after him. They're going on without him. That's why I'm leaving. They killed a family up near Jay City. I'm going up there to find them."

"Why don't you just take Rufus to Fort Smith and let Judge Parker hang him?"

"That's going to happen, Jenny," Clint said, "just not yet."

She bounded out of bed, the movement making her breasts bounce angrily. They continued to bounce while she dressed, until she covered them with her clothes.

"Jenny, don't go—"

She whirled on him.

"If he gets out and kills me, it'll be your fault."

"He's not going to get out."

"Without you here, he will," she insisted.

"So then leave here, Jenny."

"With what?" she demanded. "I got no money, and even if I did I got nowhere to go."

"Jenny—"

"Where can I go?"

She started for the door, but before she could leave he said, "Go to Jay City."

She stopped short and looked at him over her shoulder. She wiped tears from her face with the flat of her palm.

"What?"

"Come to Jay City with me," he said. "I'll put you in a hotel there, and you can get a job."

"What kind of a job?"

"Anything," he said. "You can do what you were doing here, or you can do something else."

"Jay City ain't much bigger than this."

"You can leave there, in time."

"And go where?"

"Fort Smith."

"With you?"

"I'll take you there, if you want."

She turned and faced him.

"Don't get me wrong, Jenny—"

"Relax," she said, "I don't expect you to marry me or anything."

Clint breathed a sigh of relief. He'd been starting to think that she was misunderstanding him.

"But it would help to have someone take me out of here," she said.

"We'll get you a horse and you can ride with me to Jay City. Once you're there you can decide what else you want to do."

She sniffed, rubbed her nose with her palm, and asked, "What time do we leave?"

"Early."

"How early?"

"First light."

"That's early."

"I need to get an early start."

"I ain't complainin'," she said. "I'll be ready."

"You want to stay here tonight?"

"No," she said. "Yes—I'll come back. I got to quit my job, and get my things. I'll come back."

"Okay," he said. "I'll be here."

She started to leave, then impulsively rushed him and kissed him before doing so.

"Thank you."

"You're welcome."

She left, slamming the door in her haste.

For a couple of hours after she had gone, Clint sat on the bed and went through a few scenarios in his head. The one that bothered him had the gang going to the Jay City area, killing that family, stealing the girl, and then doubling back to Carlyle when he went to Jay City. They'd come back here and get Rufus King out of jail.

He dismissed the thought. By his own admission Rufus said that no one in his gang was very smart. Clint believed that Rufus believed that. They were, however, smart enough to kill somebody while their leader was in jail. They would have had to vote on a new leader in order to do that, and Clint didn't think that a new leader would particularly want to help the old leader escape from jail.

No, they weren't going to come back here, but just in case they did, he felt better about having Jenny with him in Jay City.

She was right in what she had said. If Rufus got out and killed her, Clint would never forgive himself.

THIRTY-ONE

Jenny woke up first in the morning so Clint was helpless
to stop her when she burrowed under the covers and started
rubbing her cheek against his flaccid penis. Before he knew
what was happening, he was hard, and she was licking the
underside, up and down, until he was fully awake, and then
she engulfed him fully and sucked him until he exploded
with such force that the bed moved.

They were late leaving Carlyle, which Clint told Jenny
was completely her fault. However, they were both smiling
when they left town, he at the memory of how he had been
awakened, and she from the sheer joy she felt at leaving
the small town forever.

When they arrived in Jay City, Clint could see what Jenny
had meant. It didn't look much larger than Carlyle at first
glance, but it did have two hotels, a sheriff's office that
was open, and a busy street at ten in the morning.

"Where do we go first?" Jenny asked.

"We'll put the horses in the livery and get a hotel room.
After that I have to go and see the sheriff. You can do
whatever you want to do."

"Whatever I want?"

"It's your life. You can look for a job, or put that off and take it easy."

"I think I'll take a long, hot bath. I haven't been able to just soak in a long time."

"Good," he said, "you soak, and I'll go see the sheriff."

While Jenny was luxuriating in hot water, Clint walked to the jail and entered without knocking. The man behind the desk looked up at him and immediately recognized him as a stranger.

"What can I do for you?" the sheriff asked.

"Sheriff," he said. "I'm Clint Adams, and I've got Rufus King locked up in the Carlyle jail."

"I heard that," the man said. "I also heard that jail was closed up."

"I opened it."

"Uh-huh," the man said. "I also heard you had a badge from Judge Parker."

"I do." Clint reached into his pocket and showed the man the badge. The sheriff was in his thirties, and from the way he looked at the deputy marshal's badge he'd probably been wanting one most of his adult life.

"All right," he said. "My name's Leiter, Sheriff Felix Leiter. What can I do for you, Marshal?"

"Just Adams," Clint said. "I'm not a deputy marshal."

"But the badge—"

"It isn't legal," Clint said, tucking it away. "I wasn't sworn in."

"Why not?"

"Because I'm doing Judge Parker a favor."

"And that is?"

"Bringing in Rufus King."

"But you said he's still in the Carlyle jail."

"That's because I'm doing someone else a favor, too," Clint said.

"Who's that?"

Clint explained about Dave Borton and his boy, Scott.

"And you think the boy might be runnin' with that gang?"

"It's possible."

"If he is, he's in a lot of trouble," Leiter said.

"I heard the gang hit near here."

"Killed Sam McTeague and his wife, Lily. Took their daughter, Lexie."

"Lexie?"

"Alexis," Leiter said. "Folks around here just called her Lexie."

"I see."

"They killed Sam right off. Doc says they raped Lily first, and then killed her."

"I heard they raped the girl, too."

"We don't know that for sure," Leiter said. "All we know is that they took her."

"Were you able to pick up their trail?"

"For a while, but we lost it."

"We? Did you go out with a posse?"

"No, just me and my deputy."

"Would you take me out to the house where it happened, Sheriff?"

"You think you might see somethin' we didn't?" There was no animosity in the man's tone. He was just wondering.

"I don't know, Sheriff," Clint said. "I'd just like to take a look."

"Well, get your horse, then," the sheriff said. "I'll take you out there right now."

THIRTY-TWO

It was a small house on a plot of land that looked mostly like hard-packed dirt. There was no corral, and there didn't look like there was any farmland.

"What did this fella do for a living?" Clint asked.

"Odd jobs," the sheriff said. "Did whatever he could to keep his family together. He was a hard worker. Everybody in town liked him, his wife, and his daughter."

"And you couldn't get a posse together?"

The sheriff shrugged.

"I guess they didn't like them *that* much."

Who do you like enough to get killed for? Clint wondered. If most people looked out for themselves, why was he always out trying to help his friends? Maybe because they couldn't help themselves. No, that wasn't true. He had friends like Bat Masterson, Wyatt Earp, and when he was alive, Wild Bill Hickok, all men who could take care of themselves—but men who occasionally needed help from a friend. He went to their aid just as they, in turn, had come to his.

"Can I look inside?"

"Sure."

They dismounted and walked to the house. The door was open, hanging on one hinge. Obviously, it had been kicked open. Clint could see it in his mind. The house was three rooms, two of them bedrooms. The other one was a combination kitchen and living room. The family must have been sitting at the table for dinner when the outlaws kicked in the door. The father would have reacted with surprise, the two women probably with fear. Clint looked around, saw two pegs on the wall by the front door, where a rifle would have been. Too far away for the father to have gotten to.

They would have grabbed the father right away and, if they hadn't killed him immediately, probably put him on the floor. Then they probably took the mother into the bedroom and raped her. He walked to the bedrooms. One was neat and clean, the bed made. The other was a shambles, the bedclothes on the floor. This would have been the parents' room, the one they dragged the mother into.

Then, for whatever reason, they decided not to rape the daughter right there, but to take her with them. They killed the parents, probably right in front of the girl, and then left.

Clint wondered if Rufus King had been telling the truth about never having killed anyone. His men—his former gang—certainly didn't have that problem.

It pained Clint to think of Scott Borton with these men, possibly even taking part in what had gone on. It pained him, but not as much as it would Dave Borton, if and when he found out.

"What do you see?" the sheriff asked.

Clint looked at the man.

"Probably the same thing you do."

"I don't think so," the sheriff said, but dropped it.

They went back outside and Clint looked at the ground. There were a lot of tracks outside, more than three or four horses' worth.

"You and your deputy trample these tracks?"

The lawman looked sheepish.

"Yeah, I guess we did."

The tracks rode off, the sheriff's and the deputy's obliterating those of the gang.

"I got to get back to town," the lawman said, feeling foolish now. He wanted to get away from Clint. He saw Clint as the source of his embarrassment, rather than because of any mistakes he'd actually made.

"That's okay, Sheriff," Clint said. "I'll stay out here a while."

"All right," the lawman said. "If there's anything I can do . . ."

"There is."

"Name it."

"A girl rode into town with me. Her name's Jenny Morse. She's over at the hotel, the, uh, Jay City Hotel."

The sheriff nodded.

"One is called the Jay City Hotel, and the other the Jay House Hotel. Easy to get them mixed up."

"Well, she's at the Jay City. Would you let her know where I am so she doesn't worry?"

"Sure. She your woman?"

"No," Clint said, "Just a girl who wanted to get away from Carlyle."

"And come to Jay City? Not much of a trade-off there, I'd say."

"Maybe not," Clint said, "but she might be moving on soon. Just let her know I didn't leave town for good, would you?"

"Sure thing."

The sheriff started for his horse and Clint called out, "Sheriff?"

"Yep?" the man replied from astride his horse.

"You married?"

"No. Why?"

"Just wondering," Clint said, thinking that the man might appeal to Jenny.

''Good luck out here,'' the lawman said.

Clint looked down at the trail the sheriff and his deputy had trampled half to death and said, ''Yeah, thanks. I'll need it.''

THIRTY-THREE

He followed the trail right up to the point where the sheriff and the deputy had lost it, and he could see why. The gang had ridden through a stream, and since the sheriff and his man obviously weren't trackers, that was where they lost them. They probably shrugged, figured they did their best, and went back to town. He wondered how hard they would have tried if everyone *didn't* like this girl Lexie.

Clint rode upstream a ways, looking for the tracks where the gang had come out, and then went downstream. If they'd been real smart they would have split up and gone both up- and downstream, but eventually he found the tracks where they had come out. There were five horses, four for the gang, and one for the girl.

He thought about following the trail the rest of the way now, but it didn't look like it was going anywhere. He decided to go back to Jay City to talk to Jenny and to get some supplies before he followed this trail that led . . . who knew where?

Wherever it went, he had to be prepared to go with it.

• • •

"Listen to them," Lucky said.

He, Louis, and Sam Sampson were in one room of the shack they had found, and Cherry Boy and the girl, Lexie, were in the other.

The two of them were having sex so loud the other three could hear them.

"Who knew she'd like it so much?" Louis asked.

"And do you think he's gonna share with us?" Lucky asked.

"Rufus used to share with us," Sampson pointed out.

"Yeah, but Cherry Boy was right about one thing," Louis said. "We did all the killin'."

"Didn't hear you complainin' about it," Sampson said.

"That's because I didn't realize it until Cherry Boy brought it up."

The girl yelled, and they heard Cherry Boy grunt real loud, and then the noise stopped.

"Guess they're done," Louis said.

"And where's the money Cherry Boy's been talkin' about?" Sampson asked. "Sure wasn't any in that house."

"The money'll come," Lucky said. "He's got plans."

"Wonder what they're doin'—" Lucky began, but he stopped when the door opened. Cherry Boy appeared in the doorway, wearing his pants but bare from the waist up. He leaned against the door frame. Past him they could see Lexie on the bed. She was totally naked. Her skin was very pale, her youthful breasts small and soft, with pink nipples. She was on her knees, and she had one hand pressed down between her legs.

"That's it, boys," he said, rubbing his chest. "I can't satisfy her no more. She wants one of you."

The gang exchanged glances.

"Which one?" Lucky asked, while his brother Louis looked hopeful.

"She don't care," Cherry Boy said. "You pick."

Both the Davis boys looked at Sampson, who shook his head and said, "Not me. You boys pick."

"What?" Cherry Boy said, but he wasn't talking to them; he had turned his head to talk to the girl. Now he turned back, chuckling. "She says she'll take both of you boys at one time. You up for that?"

Lucky and Louis looked at each other, and then both of them got up and ran for the door, almost trampling Cherry Boy as they went by.

The new gang leader laughed and closed the door, then walked over and sat down at the table with Sampson.

"What's the matter with you, Sam?"

"I ain't comfortable with this."

"With what?"

Sampson looked at him.

"Leaving Rufus in jail and you becoming leader."

"You had your chance to be leader, Sam. You didn't take it."

"I don't want to be leader, Cherry Boy."

"But you don't want me to be, either," Cherry Boy said. "Is that it?"

"I got nothin' against you."

"But you're Rufus's man, is that it?"

"Well . . ."

"Then why don't you go to Carlyle and get him out of jail?"

Sampson didn't answer.

"Why don't you go and face the Gunsmith?"

No answer.

"I'll tell you why," Cherry Boy said. "Because you're not Rufus's man *that* much, are you?"

Before Sampson could answer, noises started coming from the other room. Cherry Boy turned and looked at the door.

"You know, I didn't pop no cherry in there," he told Sampson. "She'd already been broken in. You know who by?"

"No," Sampson said glumly, and he didn't care.

"Her old man," he said, laughing, "the guy everybody

in town thinks is such a nice guy. She says he crawled into her bed when she was twelve, and he's been doin' it since. She says when we killed him she just about busted out laughing.''

"And her mother?" Sampson asked. "What about her mother?''

"She wasn't too upset about her mother, either," Cherry Boy said. "Says her mother knew what her father'd been doin' and never said a thing about it.''

"That's sick.''

"You said it," Cherry Boy said. "Now she's havin' a good time with guys her own age—us!''

From the sounds she was making, and Lucky and Louis were making, they were all having a good time.

THIRTY-FOUR

Clint found Jenny in the hotel dining room, having tea.

"Tea?" he asked, sitting opposite her.

"Just because I worked in a saloon means I can't have tea?" she asked.

"Hey, take it easy," Clint said. "I didn't mean anything by it."

"I'm sorry," she said. "I just felt like having some tea."

"Have you had anything to eat?"

"No," she said. "I was going to wait for you, and then the sheriff came in and told me what you were doing."

"You should have eaten, then."

"I was too worried about you to eat."

"Why were you worried about me?"

"Well," she said, "aside from the obvious reason of not wanting you to get killed, if you *do* get killed I'm stuck here. It would be just like staying in Carlyle."

"You're not stuck anywhere, Jenny."

"We had this conversation already," she said. "What do we do now? It's not time for lunch or dinner."

He smiled, grabbed a napkin, and said, "We eat, anyway."

After the meal Jenny had some more tea and Clint had coffee.

"What happened today?" she asked.

He told her what he had found, and what he was going to do.

"When will you leave?"

"Tomorrow morning," he said. "I'll use the rest of today to pick up some supplies. Once I leave I'm not coming back until I find them."

"No matter how long it takes?"

"No matter."

"And what about Rufus?"

"I'm going to send a telegram to Judge Parker. He can have another deputy go to Carlyle to pick up Rufus and take him back to Fort Smith."

"Can I come with you?"

"No."

"Why not?"

"You'll slow me down. Why would you want to come with me while I track down this gang, anyway? I'll be on the trail, sleeping on the ground, drinking trail coffee, eating beans—"

"He'll get away."

"What?"

"Rufus. Whoever Judge Parker sends, he'll get away and then he'll come after me."

"First of all," Clint said, "I don't think that will happen. Second, even if he got away how would he know where you are? And third, if he did get away I think he'd go looking for his gang to get some revenge on them for leaving him in jail."

She bit her lip and said, "Everything you say makes sense, but I'm still scared."

"If you stay here," Clint said, "this town has law. There's a sheriff and a deputy. You already met the sheriff."

"I did."

"How was he?"

"He seemed like a decent man."

"He is," Clint said. Probably not much of a lawman, but a decent-enough fellow.

"So just stay here, Jenny, until I get back. When I do you can decide if you want to move on."

"You'll still take me?" she asked.

"If you want to go," he said, "I'll take you as far as Fort Smith. Agreed?"

She bit her lip some more, then nodded and said, "Agreed."

THIRTY-FIVE

Clint went to the general store to arrange for his supplies, then went from there to the sheriff's office to tell the man what he had found and what he was going to do about it. When he entered, he found Sheriff Leiter in the office with a young man who was wearing a deputy's badge on his leather vest.

"Clint Adams, this is my deputy, Ken Brett."

"It's a real pleasure, Mr. Adams," Brett said, shaking Clint's hand vigorously.

"The pleasure's mine, Deputy," Clint said, reclaiming his hand from the enthusiastic young man with some effort.

"What did you find out there?" the sheriff asked.

"Well, actually, Sheriff, I found their trail. I'm going back out tomorrow to follow it wherever it leads."

"Well, I'm glad to hear that," Leiter said. "Kenny and I ain't no great trackers, so we weren't able to find the trail again."

"How'd you do it?" Brett asked.

Clint explained about the gang going into the stream and how he'd ridden up and down the opposite bank until he found where they had come out.

149

"Gosh, that was smart," Brett said.

"Just common sense," Clint said, then added, to take the sting out of it, "but you fellas have other responsibilities here in town. You can't be going off to follow some gang's trail, not knowing where it's going to take you."

"Out of our jurisdiction, probably," Leiter said.

"I don't doubt that, Sheriff," Clint said. "That's why I'm prepared to follow it to the end."

"Well, I wish you luck," Leiter said. "What are you gonna do about Rufus King?"

"After I leave here I'm going to send Judge Parker a telegram. He can send another deputy or two to Carlyle to take King back to Fort Smith. Apparently, his gang is just going to go on without him. I can't take him back to Fort Smith and forget about it, not in good conscience."

"I understand."

"I'll be leaving first thing in the morning," Clint said. "If I find them and the girl is . . . all right, I'll be bringing her back here before I take them on to Fort Smith."

"To tell you the truth, Mr. Adams," Leiter said, "you might just as well go straight on to Fort Smith. She's got no family here to come back to."

"Well," Clint said, "maybe I'll just let her decide that on her own."

He shook hands with both men again, then left to go to the telegraph office.

Somehow, when he came out of the telegraph office and found Deputy Brett standing there, he wasn't surprised.

"What can I do for you, Deputy?"

"You can take me with you, sir."

"Why would I want to do that?"

"I can help you," Brett said. "After all, there are four of them, aren't there?"

"At least."

"And one of you. Taking me with you would cut down the odds."

"Son, how long you been a deputy?"

The young man fidgeted and said, "Four months."

"How old are you?"

"Twenty-one . . . next month."

"Not much older than the boys I'm chasing," Clint said. "Are you prepared to kill one of these boys who are about your age?"

"Sir," Brett said, "I'm prepared to do whatever it takes to bring them to justice."

"And how does the sheriff feel about this?"

"If I go with you," Brett said, "I'll give my badge to the sheriff."

"You'll resign?"

"Yes, sir."

"Do you think he'll take you back when we return?"

"I figure it's time to move on anyway, sir," Brett said. "If we bring them boys into Fort Smith, I figured to light there a while."

"You think maybe Judge Parker will give you a badge if you help me?"

"To be honest, sir," Brett said, "I was thinking that might happen, yeah."

"Well, you're right," Clint said. "It might. Judge Parker is sometimes real quick to hang a badge on somebody. He needs men that badly."

"I'll do exactly what you tell me when you tell me, Mr. Adams. I figure I can learn an awful lot from a man like you."

"I'll tell you one thing," Clint said. "You're saying all the right things, boy."

"Sir," Brett said, "I ain't gonna beg you, I'm just making the offer."

"Well, if you were to be at the livery in the morning when I got there, with your horse all saddled, I'd probably let you come with me."

Brett smiled. "Thank you, sir."

"I'll be leaving at first light."

"I'll be there!" Brett said.

The young man seemed very ready for a change in his life, and Clint thought it wouldn't be too bad to have some company on the ride. Somebody to collect firewood and see to the horses, somebody who'd do everything he told him to do.

It had been a long time since he'd ridden with somebody like that.

THIRTY-SIX

Jenny seemed intent on doing everything in her power that night to kill Clint in bed so that he wouldn't be able to leave.

"Jesus, woman," he said, while she was between his legs, sucking on him, "I've got to get some sleep."

He propped himself up on an elbow, and she just reached up with one hand and pushed him back down into the mattress and continued using her mouth and tongue on him until he lifted his butt off the bed and came with a loud roar. . . .

In the morning his legs were wobbly as he dressed while she watched him.

"Well," he said, "if I could survive last night I can survive anything."

"Well, if last night doesn't keep you here, nothing will," she said. "You just better be real careful and come back."

He kissed her quickly and said, "I intend to do both. You take care of yourself while I'm gone. If you need anything check in with the sheriff."

"I will," she said, and then lay back on the bed and

stretched so he could watch all the muscles in her naked body bunch and move. "In fact, maybe I'll get real friendly with the sheriff while you're gone."

"Now that would be real nice, Jenny," he said. "And safe. I mean, if you were in bed with the law nobody could bother you."

"You'd like me to go to bed with him, wouldn't you?" she asked. "You wouldn't even be jealous."

"I don't have a jealous bone in my body," Clint said. "I told you before, it's your life. What you do with it is up to you."

He went out the door; after he'd closed it, he heard something crash against it. He didn't know what it was, but he figured he was going to have to pay for it.

When he got to the livery stable, Kenny Brett was there, holding the reins on a sturdy-looking steeldust.

"Nice horse," Clint said.

"He'll do."

"How did the sheriff take your resignation?"

"He didn't accept it," Brett said. "He just told me to leave the badge behind and it would be here waiting for me if and when I got back."

"He's a decent man."

"He's a good man, all right," Brett said. "Took me on when I had no experience."

"Well, wait here and I'll saddle up and join you. Oh, here." Clint handed the younger man a sack.

"What's this?"

"We're traveling light," Clint told him, "but you can carry the supplies."

Brett grinned and tied the sack around his saddle horn, letting it hang there.

Clint saddled Duke and hoped he was doing the right thing by bringing the younger man along. This way, it seemed, he'd have the lives of two young men hanging in the balance—Scott Borton and Kenny Brett.

Well, he thought, mounting up, *if I'd thought of that yesterday I probably would have told him no, but it's too late for that now.*

He rode outside and asked, "Ready?"

"More than ready."

"I don't want you to be more than ready, Kenny," Clint said. "I don't want you to do more than I ask you. Do you understand what I'm saying?"

"Yes, sir," Brett said. "You just want me to do what you tell me, when you tell me."

"You remember that," Clint said, "and we're going to get along just fine."

THIRTY-SEVEN

"Well," Kenny Brett said, staring at the stream, "we managed to get this far."

"I rode upstream first," Clint said, pointing that way, "and then downstream. Come on, I'll show you what I found."

Brett followed Clint into the stream, and they rode down to the point where the tracks came out of the water.

"Look at that," Brett said, staring at the tracks. "Why didn't we see that?"

"I guess you didn't look," Clint said. "Did either of you ride into the stream?"

"As a matter of fact, we did," Brett said. "The sheriff rode upstream, and I rode down here. So I'm the one who missed it." Brett looked forlorn.

"Don't feel too bad," Clint said. "Anyone could have missed it."

"But it wasn't anyone who missed it," Brett said. "It was me, and it was my job to find it."

"Well," Clint said, "let's follow them and see where they lead."

•   •   •

Lucky Davis came out of the room breathing hard. His brother Louis went in and closed the door behind him.

"Is that all she does?" Sam Sampson asked.

"I'm not complaining," Lucky said. "Maybe when you're introduced to it as young as she was it gets to be—I don't know, habit-forming?"

"You'd think her thighs would chafe, or something," Sampson said.

"Well," Lucky said, "we're not always between her thighs, are we?"

Sampson made a face.

"Why don't you go in for a while, Sam?"

"Too many ahead of me," Sampson said.

"You never minded going in after Rufus."

"Rufus was my friend."

"And we're not?"

Sampson looked at Lucky and said, "No, you're not."

Lucky frowned, then looked around.

"Where's Cherry Boy?"

"Where do you think?"

"I don't know why he doesn't quit that job," Lucky said. "Seems silly to me. How's he gonna be our leader and keep working for—"

"He's not," Sampson said, standing abruptly.

"What? He's not what?"

"He's not my leader."

"What do you mean? Where are you goin'?"

"I'm gonna do what we should've done a long time ago," Sampson said, heading for the door.

"What's that?"

"Get Rufus out of jail."

"By yourself?"

"By myself."

"Cherry Boy's not gonna like this!" Lucky called after him.

"Fuck Cherry Boy!" Sampson said, and left.

Lucky looked around the room for a moment, then was

attracted to the other room by the noises his brother and Lexie were making. He forgot all about Sam Sampson.

Sam Sampson saddled his horse, shaking his head the whole time. When Rufus was in charge they never sat around some shack for days, taking turns with a sixteen-year-old girl who couldn't get enough. He wanted things back the way they were, and that meant getting Rufus out of jail. Rufus could take care of Cherry Boy, then, and things would get back to normal.

THIRTY-EIGHT

"These tracks are still pretty clear," Ken Brett said, sometime later. "Even I can see them."

"The ground's pretty soft here," Clint said. "This is very careless of the gang."

"Is it?"

Clint nodded.

"I don't think they would have left tracks like this if Rufus King was still leading them."

"King would be too smart for this?"

"I'm sure he would."

"Where do you suppose they lead?"

"I don't know," Clint said, "but wherever it is I think we'll find our gang. I just hope that young girl is still alive."

"A pretty thing like that," Brett said. "Why would they kill her?"

"Sick bastards like that?" Clint replied. "Who knows why they do anything?"

"Do you think Rufus King is a sick bastard, too?"

"Rufus? No, he was just out to have some fun. The rest of them, they're sick."

"Why's that?"

"They did all the killings," Clint said.

"Is that what Rufus said?"

Clint nodded again. "He was too smart to kill anyone himself, so he always had one of them do it. Unfortunately for him, that's not going to carry much weight with Judge Parker."

"It won't?"

"He'll hang him anyway."

"Well," Brett said, "even if he didn't shoot anyone, or stab anyone, or step on their neck, he was still responsible, wasn't he?"

"I suppose he was," Clint said, thoughtfully.

Sometime later they came within sight of a shack. There was a lean-to off to one side with horses in it, three of them.

"Somebody's missing," Brett said.

"Two somebodies," Clint replied. "There's four men, and the girl. Five horses. There are only three in that lean-to. Dismount, we'll go the rest of the way on foot."

"No one on lookout," Brett observed.

"More carelessness," Clint said. "Their own stupidity is going to put them at the end of a rope."

"Maybe not."

Clint didn't have to turn to know that the "deputy" was holding a gun on him.

"How about your stupidity?" Brett asked.

"I'm not stupid."

"No? What do you call getting caught like this?"

"Not surprising," Clint said.

"You're gonna try to tell me this ain't a surprise?" Brett asked.

"That's right."

"You knew all along that I was part of the gang?"

"Not all along," Clint said. "Just since the stream."

"Why?"

"Because," Clint said, "you're riding the same horse you rode the first time you went into that stream. You made the same tracks coming out. See what I mean about carelessness?"

"Well, how about I just shoot you in the back and leave you here because of *your* carelessness?"

"You won't do that."

"Why won't I?"

"Because you want your friends in the shack to witness it. You want them to see you shoot me."

"You're pretty smart, all right," Brett said. "Let's go, Mr. Gunsmith. Let's get it over with."

THIRTY-NINE

As soon as they entered the shack both Clint and Brett could hear the rutting sounds from the other room.

"Goddamn, but that girl never gets enough," Brett said with a smile.

"Is that . . . Lexie?" Clint asked. The girl was crying out, and it wasn't in pain.

"Sure is."

Brett walked to the door and, keeping an eye on Clint, kicked it open.

"Come on out here, boys. Bring little Lexie. There's somebody I want you to meet."

"We ain't done!" somebody yelled.

"I said get out here!"

"Awright."

Two men who looked enough alike to be brothers came out, both pulling on their pants, naked from the waist up, and barefoot.

"What's goin' on, Cherry Boy?" Lucky asked.

Clint felt relief flood through him. If Ken Brett was "Cherry Boy," then Scott Borton couldn't be.

"Lexie, come on out here, honey," Brett/Cherry Boy called.

The girl came to the doorway stark naked. Clint couldn't take his eyes off of her. She was a beautiful girl, and would no doubt grow to be a beautiful woman. Her body was not fully developed, and yet she had lovely breasts, small but solid, with pink nipples. She was gnawing on a thumbnail as she looked out from beneath blond bangs at Clint.

"Who's he?" she asked. "I ain't gonna do it with him."

"Why not?" Brett asked. "This here's the famous Clint Adams. He came to save you."

She giggled and said, "I don't need no savin', mister. I'm fine right where I am."

"Lexie, didn't these boys kill your parents and kidnap you?"

"So what?" she asked. "I like it better here than I ever did at home."

"See," Brett explained, "she likes what we give her better than what her daddy used to give her."

"You mean—"

"Yep," Brett said. "Daddy's the one what broke her in. Did it when she was twelve, been doin' it ever since—till we killed him."

"Jesus," Clint muttered. "Well, all right, it's time to go."

"What?" Brett asked.

"You heard me," Clint said. "Time to go to town. You're all goin' to jail."

"Me, too?" Lexie asked.

"Not you, Lexie."

"Can one of them stay here and, ya know, keep doin' it with me?"

"I'm afraid not, Lexie."

"Shoot," she said, and leaned against the door frame, one leg hooked behind the other. She was totally unself-conscious about her nudity.

"Why don't you put some clothes on, Lexie?" Clint asked.

"That one don't belong in jail," Brett said, "she belongs in a whorehouse. She'd be a goddamned moneymaker."

"I'll take her someplace where she'll be taken care of," Clint said, "after I take you three to jail."

"Now, I think you're a little mixed-up, Mr. Gunsmith," Brett said.

"Is that a fact?"

"Sure is," Brett said. "See, I got the gun on you."

"But you made a big mistake, Kenny," Clint said. "You've been making them all along, but this one is the biggest."

"And what's that?"

"I still have my gun."

Lucky and Louis Davis stared at Clint, and then looked at his holster. They had simply assumed that Brett/Cherry Boy had disarmed the man.

"Shit!" Lucky said.

"Why didn't you take his gun?" Louis demanded.

"What's the difference?" Brett asked. "I got my gun pointed at him. What's he gonna do?"

"Damn," Lucky said, "we need our guns."

Lucky and Louis started to turn back into the other room, but Clint stopped them.

"Stand fast, boys!" he shouted. "You don't need your guns."

"We don't?" Lucky asked.

"They'll only get you killed," Clint said. "You're going to stay alive simply because you're unarmed."

"W-what about him?" Louis asked, indicating Ken Brett.

"Him? He's a dead man, unless he puts his gun down," Clint said.

Brett started to laugh, then stopped and frowned.

"I don't get it," he said, looking at Clint. "I'm pointing my gun at you." He said it slowly, as if he were speaking to a child. "Do you see it?" He waggled it back and forth.

"I see it," Clint said, "but what you don't understand is that I can draw my gun and fire it before you can pull the trigger."

"Naw," Brett said. "You ain't that fast. Nobody is that fast."

"You willing to bet your life on that?" Clint asked. "Because I am."

FORTY

It was tense and quiet—so quiet that they could hear the girl in the next room, humming to herself. Clint had the feeling that this girl was going to have a hard time as an adult if she didn't get some help. She seemed to him to be in some kind of shock, but he had no time right then to worry about her.

He couldn't believe that Ken Brett had been too stupid to take his gun. Of course, he had allowed the boy to get the drop on him, assuming that he wouldn't want to kill him without an audience. That assumption had been correct, but now he was facing a drawn gun, and he had two choices: talk the boy out of shooting him, or draw against a drawn gun. He could count the times he'd done that successfully on the fingers of one hand.

"What's it going to be, Ken?" Clint asked. "Or should I call you Cherry Boy, the way these idiots do?"

"Hey—" Louis started, but his brother quieted him with a clipped, "Shut up!"

Clint had a feeling that whatever happened once the action started, the two brothers would run into the other room for their guns. He'd have to catch them before they got to them.

"Kenny . . ." Clint said.

"I'm thinking!" Brett snapped. His hand flexed around the gun nervously, again and again. At one point, for an instant, his trigger finger was out of position for an easy pull. Clint kept his eyes on the boy's hands.

"That's good, Kenny," Clint said, "because if you're thinking that means you're still alive."

"You can't draw on me and win . . . you can't," Brett said.

"Don't make me prove it, boy," Clint said. "Put the gun down."

Brett licked his lips and looked at the Davis boys. In that moment Clint drew, but he held his instincts in check and didn't fire. He couldn't remember the last time he'd drawn that way and not fired.

Kenny Brett jumped in place, startled by the move, and one of the Davis brothers said, "Shit."

"Now we're even, Kenny," Clint said. "I could have killed you, but I didn't. Drop the gun."

Brett was undecided.

"Drop it!"

"Shoot him!" Lucky Davis yelled, and turned to run into the other room, followed by his brother.

Abruptly, Ken Brett released his gun as if it had suddenly become hot.

"Stay there," Clint said, "and stay smart."

He sprinted for the door. As he entered the room both brothers were drawing their guns from their holsters. He had no choice but to fire and did so, twice. One of them got his hand around his gun and fired it once, just before he died. The bullet hit the girl before she knew what was happening, and drilled her neatly through the left breast. She stopped humming.

Clint knew he'd drilled both boys dead center. Normally

he'd have checked them anyway, but he didn't want to forget about Brett in the other room.

He went back out and the ex-deputy was still standing there, stunned.

"I ain't never seen nothin' . . . that fast," he said.

Clint holstered his gun, walked over to the boy and kicked his gun away, then backhanded him across the face. Brett fell on his ass.

"I don't have time to impress you," Clint said. "What happened to the boy named Scott Borton?"

"Huh?" Brett looked up at him, his eyes unfocused.

Clint reached down and hauled him to his feet by his shirtfront.

"Scott Borton! Did you know him?"

"I don't know nobody by that name," he said.

"He was with the gang."

"Not when I joined them," Brett said. "Maybe Sampson knows."

"Who?"

"Sam Sampson," Brett said. "He's the one who's missing."

"Where do you think he went, Kenny?"

"That's easy," Brett said, blood trickling down his chin from his mouth. "He was all for busting Rufus out of jail in Carlyle. That's probably where he went."

"All right, then," Clint said, "let's go."

"Where you takin' me?"

"Back to town," Clint said. "I'm going to turn you over to your boss, and then I'm going back to Carlyle."

FORTY-ONE

"I can't believe it."

Sheriff Leiter had just locked the cell with Kenny Brett in it, and he still held the key in his hand.

"I thought Kenny was okay," he said. "I never suspected—and Lexie! Poor kid."

"You never know what's going on inside somebody's home, Sheriff."

"And now she's dead," Leiter said, shaking his head. "Ah, who knows. Maybe she's better off. She must have been . . . well, out of her head if what you say about her is true. Those bastards!"

He finally hung the key back on the wall hook, but with such force that he almost pulled the hook out of the wall.

"What are you going to do now?" Leiter asked him.

"I'm going back to Carlyle," he said. "My only chance is to stop Sampson before he kills somebody or gets killed trying to break Rufus King out of jail."

"You think he's gonna tell you about the Borton boy?" Leiter asked.

"I hope so," Clint said, "because I don't think Rufus King ever will. He's too mean."

"What about, uh, your friend? I mean, the girl."

"She'll stay here," Clint said. "She won't want to go back. Can I ask you to look after her a little longer?"

Leiter's face colored and he stammered, "Uh, well, s-sure, I can do that."

Clint smiled. It was clear the sheriff was smitten.

"I'll let her know," he said, and headed for the door.

"What about Kenny?"

At the door Clint turned and said, "I'll have the same deputies who pick up Rufus King stop here and pick him up, too."

"Looks like you did what you set out to do," Leiter said. "Break up the King gang."

"I haven't done everything I set out to do," Clint said, and left the office.

Sampson had been in no great hurry to get to Carlyle. Rufus wasn't going anywhere, and he enjoyed being away from the Davis brothers, and from Cherry Boy, and even from the girl. Her eyes scared him, and as pretty as she was he hadn't liked looking at her.

He didn't know what he was going to do when he got to Carlyle. Guess he'd have to find out if Clint Adams was still there, or if he'd gone out looking for the rest of the gang.

It sure would help things if he didn't have to face the Gunsmith.

Rufus King had not yet resigned himself to hanging. Adams was gone, a marshal had not yet arrived, and he was being guarded by two men who—he thought—were afraid of him. Sooner or later, his chance would come.

Clint found Jenny and told her what he was going to do.

"I'm not going back," she said.

"I didn't think you would," he answered. "Stay here and wait, or go on to Fort Smith."

"I'll wait."

"The sheriff will look after you."

"He wants to do more than that," she said, "and maybe I'll let him."

Clint shook his head as he left the hotel. He didn't know if she was madder at him for leaving, or for not caring if she *did* let the sheriff do more than that.

FORTY-TWO

Clint's ride to Carlyle was much faster than Sam Sampson's had been. Consequently, the outlaw did not get there that much ahead of him. Instead of riding to the livery Clint rode straight to the jailhouse and knocked on the door.

"Who is it?" Roy Jackson called out.

"It's Clint Adams."

He heard the door being unlocked and then it swung open. Jackson stood there with Carl Everett's shotgun.

"Didn't expect to see you for a while."

"I'm not coming in," Clint said. "One of King's gang is in town and I'm going to find him. Lock the door and keep it locked. Don't open it for anyone but me."

"What about Carl?"

"Anyone but me, got it?"

"Okay," Jackson said with a shrug. "I was gettin' tired of playin' checkers, anyway."

Clint waited while Jackson closed the door and locked it. Then, armed with Sam Sampson's description from Ken Brett, he started walking, looking for the man.

• • •

Sampson had discovered that Clint Adams wasn't in town. By hanging around the saloon he also found out that two men were taking turns guarding Rufus, and that one of them was a storekeeper. He decided to wait until the storekeeper was in the jail to make his move.

He was nursing a beer in the saloon where Jenny Morse used to work when Clint Adams walked in. Sampson froze. He didn't think Adams knew what he looked like, so he just stood as still as possible, willing himself to become invisible.

It didn't help. There were only a few men in the saloon and Sampson was the only one who fit his own description. Young, tall, red-haired.

Clint walked to the bar and ordered a beer.

"And give my friend another one," Clint said. "He's going to need it."

"Who?" Sampson asked. "Me?"

"That's right, son, you," Clint said. "I just came from Jay City, where Ken Brett—the fella you call Cherry Boy—told me what you looked like."

"Cherry Boy?"

"That's right," Clint said. "He's in jail there."

Sampson tried to swallow but his mouth was dry. When the bartender put the fresh beer in front of him, he grabbed it and drank half.

"And the other two members of your gang? The Davis brothers? They're dead."

"Dead?"

"And so's the girl," Clint said. "Too bad about that. She caught a stray bullet from one of them."

Clint sipped his own beer, giving his story time to sink in.

"So you see," he went on, "you're the only one left."

Sampson tried once to brazen it out.

"Mister, I don't know what—"

"Oh, don't try that, Sampson," Clint said, disgusted. "At least have the good sense to know when it's over.

Rufus is in jail, Brett's in jail, the others are dead, and you have a choice.''

"A . . . choice?''

"That's right,'' Clint said. "You can join Rufus and Brett, or you can join the Davis brothers. That's your choice.''

"L-look—''

"No, you look,'' Clint said. "You came here to get Rufus out of jail. That's not going to happen. The best you can do is keep yourself alive. Do you know how to do that?''

"H-how?''

"Take your gun out slowly and slide it down the bar to me.''

Sampson hesitated.

"Come on,'' Clint said. "Do it, if you want to stay alive. Either slide it here or use it.''

"Jeez,'' Sampson said. He sure didn't want to draw on the Gunsmith. He took the gun out and slid it to Clint.

"Good man.''

Clint took the gun and tucked it into his belt.

"Now we're going to walk over to the jail, but before we do that you're going to tell me something I want to know.''

"What's that?''

"I want you to tell me where Scott Borton is.''

"Borton?''

"That's right.''

"I don't know—''

"He's a young man who joined your gang near Muskogee. He's tall, blond . . .''

"Oh,'' Sampson said, then swallowed. "Him.''

"That's right,'' Clint said. "Him. Where is he?''

"He—he didn't join our gang.''

"He didn't?''

Sampson shook his head.

"Then what happened?''

Sampson swallowed and said, "He's dead."

Clint's heart sank. He didn't know if this was better or worse than having the boy be part of the gang.

"How did it happen?"

"Rufus killed him."

"Rufus killed him? Are you sure?"

"Sure I'm sure," Sampson said. "I was there. The Borton kid was saying how wrong we were to do what we was doin', and Rufus got mad and shot him."

"Rufus says he never killed anyone, that he let you fellas do all the killing."

"That's true," Sampson said, "except for that kid. I'm the only one who saw it. The others didn't know, and Rufus didn't want them to know."

"Now, this is important, Sam," Clint said, "so listen to the question. You're going to tell all of this to Judge Parker, aren't you?"

Sampson swallowed and said, "Yes, sir."

"Because it might—I'm not sure, mind you—but it might save you from hanging with Rufus."

"Yes, sir."

"Where's the body?"

"We buried it," Sampson said, "Rufus and me, right near Muskogee."

"Can you describe to me where he's buried?"

"I think so."

"Then do it, son," Clint said. "Do it now while I'm still in a good mood, because I've got to tell you I don't have much more regard for you for watching Rufus kill Scott than I do for Rufus."

"I told him not to—"

"Never mind that; just tell me where the body is, and we'll take a walk over to the jail. Rufus will be glad to see you. He thought all of you had forgotten about him."

"I didn't forget," Sampson said. "Maybe the others did, but I didn't."

"You're real loyal," Clint said in disgust. "Real loyal. Now start talkin'. . . ."

EPILOGUE

Clint watched Dave Borton kneel by his son's grave and put flowers on it. All the time he'd been worried that his son had joined Rufus King and his gang, the boy's body had been lying under the ground just a few miles away from his home.

When Clint had brought Sam Sampson over to the jail and put him in the cell next to Rufus King, they'd had a fine old reunion. Sampson told Rufus what had happened while he was locked up, and then told him everything Clint had told him in the saloon.

He didn't tell Rufus that he'd told Clint about Scott Borton, or that he'd agreed to talk to Judge Parker to save his own neck. If he had, Clint didn't think they would have had such a fine old reunion.

Clint had waited a day until two of Judge Parker's official deputies arrived, and then he turned both Sampson and Rufus King over to them. After that he rode back to Muskogee to talk to Dave Borton . . .

"I knew my boy was no outlaw," Borton had said, when Clint gave him the news.

"No, he wasn't, Dave," Clint agreed. "He was trying to talk those boys out of what they were doing when Rufus King shot him."

"I guess I shouldn't feel relieved," Borton said, "but at least now I know where he is, and that he wasn't runnin' with them scum."

"I think you knew that all along, Dave."

"Yeah, maybe," Borton said, "but I got you to thank for provin' it to me, Clint."

After that, Clint had taken Borton to the grave site, after first making sure that Sampson had given him the right location.

Borton stood up and walked back to where Clint was waiting.

"I thought about diggin' him up and burying him closer to home. But I want him to rest in peace."

"I'm sure he is, Dave."

"You comin' back to the house, Clint?"

"No," he replied, "I've got to get to Jay City. I've got a gal waiting there who might want to go to Fort Smith, if she and the sheriff haven't made friends by now. And I've got to go to Fort Smith anyway to give Judge Parker back his badge."

Borton put out his hand and said, "You thank Judge Parker for me for pullin' you into this."

"I'll thank him for you, Dave," Clint said, shaking the man's hand, "because I sure as hell had no intention of thanking him for myself."

Watch for

MAXIMILIAN'S TREASURE

210th novel in the exciting GUNSMITH series
from Jove

Coming in July!

Explore the exciting Old West with one of the men who made it wild!